Let's Skip This Christmas

JENNIFER NICE

1

Anna

'Of course,' said Anna. 'Of course you sent me this way.' She gave her SatNav a look. 'Don't try and blame this on me,' she told it. 'I looked at a map before I left. I may not have understood it, but I looked. And I checked the route planner. It's not my fault I forgot it when the time came. And I checked the weather. They didn't mention snow.'

That last bit was a lie. The weather app had mentioned snow, but light snow, which was what had started falling on the motorway. Not these heavy flurries of large snowflakes that made it almost impossible to see out of her windscreen. Anna hadn't noticed any weather warnings. She should have known, but if the qualified meteorologists didn't know, what chance did she have?

And when did it snow at Christmas? Never! It

never snowed at Christmas.

It was just Anna's luck that it decided to snow the year she decided to drive herself north and have a Christmas all to herself. It couldn't have waited until she was at the cottage and settled with her food delivery. Oh no.

Still, Anna was looking on the bright side.

It was snowing!

At Christmas!

If she wasn't driving, she'd do a little happy squeal and dance right there in the car.

It could have been worse. She had a blanket and food in the back of the car, her boots in the passenger seat footwell beside her and, according to the SatNav, she was an hour away. Of course, the SatNav was proving suspiciously untrustworthy right now.

Trundling down the narrow country road, praying nothing would come the other way, Anna followed the SatNav's instructions and breathed a sigh of relief when a proper road came into sight. Once on it, she turned into a layby, kept the engine and heater running, and had a stern talk with the SatNav on the car's screen.

Figuring out where she was, Anna looked at the route ahead. By the time she raised her eyes to the road, nearly everything was white. Her stomach dropped.

'Maybe this isn't such a good idea.' Oh, but the cottage and the log burner and the cosiness, and just her and a tree and some good food with the TV and a roaring fire. And now the snow outside.

That was the Christmas Anna wanted.

Sighing, she considered her options.

It was another hour to the cottage, through heavy snow. Or she could turn back and go home, driving for three hours in heavy snow on the motorway, which would probably be at a standstill somewhere down the line. She didn't fancy that. Who did?

The other option was to find a nearby hotel and hope the snow thawed overnight. Staring out of the window, Anna silently proposed the question to the heavy grey sky.

It didn't reply.

Blowing out her cheeks, Anna put her car into gear.

Onward it was. Onward to the Christmas she'd been planning for the last three months.

Just before she could pull out onto the road, her phone pinged. Sitting back, she quickly checked it. Just in case it was an emergency, or the government telling everyone that the end was nigh and to eat your turkey now.

Nope.

Her supermarket food delivery had been delayed.

Sucking on her lower lip, Anna looked at the timings. It would be fine. She had the backup food in her car, because she'd had a feeling this might happen.

She tucked her phone away and continued, crunching out onto the quiet road and carefully picking up as much speed as she dared, windscreen wipers working furiously against the growing flurries.

Around twenty minutes in, the loud Christmas music quietened for an embarrassing moment to allow her phone to ping again. Anna shut her mouth quickly as the car was filled with her loud singing voice instead of the music.

It was okay. Her windows were shut and there weren't many people around to have heard her. In fact, there was no one walking on the pavements either side of the road, and only a few cars, presumably drivers who had been caught out like her. A bus went past at one point with almost no one on board.

Where was everyone?

This had all happened so fast, how had so many people been presumably prepared? Had Anna missed the big snow announcement?

She supposed it wasn't so unusual for a predicted shower to turn into a full-on deluge, but when that happened, people got caught in it.

Sighing, she leaned forward into the steering wheel and had a proper look through the snow, turning the music down a little so she could see better.

Forty minutes in, the snow lessened a little and

Anna relaxed. Everything was going to be okay.

Until the SatNav pointed her down another narrow road. Instead of turning, Anna went past it, found a place to pull over and did some more digital recon.

The road led to a village, on the other side of which was the cottage. She was nearly there. But there had to be a better road to get there.

She swiped and zoomed in and out. No. That was the road into the village. In which case, it couldn't be that narrow and scary. She'd probably be all right.

There was a new message on her phone and Anna opened it with eyes narrowed against the bad news that her shopping wouldn't be delivered. Instead, it was from her mother.

Are you there yet? The snow is on the news! Let me know you're ok.

Anna smiled and hit out a reply.

I'm nearly there. The snow is bad but everything's ok. I'll let you know when I'm there. Won't be long.

'Yes, Mum,' Anna murmured as her mother replied.

Be careful.

She put the phone away, turned the car around and took the turning. At first there were only high hedges and fields on either side of her, on a road just wide enough for two cars to pass. Heavens help her if a tractor or a lorry came towards her. Although a tractor wouldn't be so bad – it would probably be ploughing the snow.

After that thought, she urged a tractor to come out from one of the fields and trundle along in front of her, clearing the path for both of them.

No tractors appeared. Neither did lorries. There were a couple of cars, and Anna found it a relief to see other people out in the world.

Eventually, houses began to appear. A farmhouse there, a bungalow here, and then a road of period terraces. She was getting close to the village.

Another turning and her car spluttered.

Anna stared down at the steering wheel in surprise.

'What was that?' she asked the car. 'Don't you dare even think about it. You can do this. It's only a bit of snow. A bit of cold. Don't fail me now, car. We're so nearly there. Just think, a Christmas to ourselves. No kids screaming at me or forcing me to play after I've just eaten, no babysitting, no being asked why I'm still single or when I'm going to sort my life out, or how my stupid job is stupid going. Just you and me and a nice cottage and yummy food. When it gets delivered. Yeah? So come on. You got this.'

As if responding to the motivational talk, the car gave a little roar and pottered down the road laden with thick snow.

'Atta car,' Anna whispered, stroking the steering wheel with her thumb.

She held her breath when it spluttered again, giving a tremble this time.

'No, no, no, no. Please. We're so close.'

The engine cut out.

Heart pounding, Anna pulled the car over with the last of its life, straight into a snow pile. Which probably wasn't the best of ideas, but given the narrowness of the road, she wasn't sure what else to do.

With the engine off, the heater was also off. Anna immediately began shivering as the cold snaked its way in, the snow already heaping on the windscreen now that the wipers weren't working to fend it off.

'This is not happening,' Anna mumbled, finding her phone and looking for the number of the breakdown service. When she tried to call it, nothing happened.

Anna stared at her phone for a moment and then swore loudly.

There was no reception.

Staring out into the freezing white, narrow landscape around her, once again, Anna considered her choices.

'Probably should have turned back and gotten stuck on the motorway,' she muttered. 'At least I wouldn't have frozen to death. At least, not as quickly.' She mentally shook herself. 'Come on.

This is nothing. And it's Christmas! Time for a miracle.'

She stared at her phone screen, but the reception bars remained stubbornly lacking.

Growling, Anna swapped her shoes for the boots and dragged her coat from the backseat. It took some time to get the car door open, pushing against the drift of thick snow.

The falling snowflakes hit her immediately in a wall of frozen water. Pulling her coat tight about her, a snowflake flying straight into her eye, she looked up and down the road.

Maybe someone would come along and she could wave them down for help. Although they wouldn't have reception either, so what would be the point?

A heater, whispered the voice in her head. Heat would be nice.

She nodded to herself and made a decision.

A little way up the road were two houses. One was strewn with Christmas lights, so Anna went there first, climbing up the long driveway, snow crunching and slipping beneath her feet. She rang the doorbell and waited, bouncing up and down on her toes.

When no answer came, she knocked and rang the bell again.

Finally, admitting defeat, she considered the large house next door. It was double-fronted with an Edwardian design and surrounded by tall trees.

The garden had been loved once, but not in recent years. Rose bushes grew along the edge of the drive-way. At the top, Anna paused to study one perfectly frozen red rose. Every cell in her body demanded that she touch it, but she resisted for fear of the flower falling apart.

The house wasn't decorated, but there in a corner window, a light was on.

Breathing a cloudy sigh of relief, Anna knocked on the door and waited.

Nothing happened.

Maybe the person who lived there moved slowly. So she waited a little more, and then knocked again, harder this time. There wasn't a bell, unless you counted the actual bell hanging by the side of the door. Anna considered ringing it but decided against it. If they couldn't hear a knock, they wouldn't hear a random bell outside.

Anna smirked to herself. Unless they thought it was Santa. They'd probably open the door for Santa.

She was just reaching up to give the bell a ring when the front door opened and Anna froze, snow falling heavily behind her, sending shivers down her back. The rest of her was protected by the porch, but the walk from the car had left her covered and now she stood, arm reaching up, eyes swivelling to the figure in the doorway, as snow dripped down through her hair to the end of her nose.

The man in the doorway was taller than her with broad shoulders and an equally broad chest, a flop of brown hair, hard chestnut eyes beneath questioning eyebrows, and a mouth that Anna couldn't take her eyes from.

She'd expected someone elderly. Preferably elderly and helpful, with a landline, and maybe some fresh mince pies.

What she'd gotten was a man far too attractive considering the state of her.

Anna lowered her arm and cleared her throat, trying to remember the explanation she'd devised and practised on the way up the driveway.

2

Ben

When he'd last looked out of the window, light snowflakes had started to fall. It gave Ben quite a shock when he next looked up from his computer to peer out of the window and found the world had turned white. Wheeling his office chair back, he stood and leaned over the windowsill to get a proper look. The snow was still falling, heavier now, with thicker snowflakes. Ben shivered and then came the realisation that the room had become quite dark. Flicking on the light, he grabbed his coffee cup and walked through the house to the kitchen. The window onto the back garden entertained him while the coffee machine did its thing. The snow was piling up. He should be checking the road and his car, but he had nowhere to be. Still, he wished he'd put the car in the garage. He should have stopped to think when he saw the first signs of snow, but the forecast hadn't been for this kind of weather.

Ben took his coffee and a couple of biscuits back to his office. Before he could collapse into his chair, he went to check what the roads were like, peering through the upstairs window.

There would be no leaving the house for a while, but that suited Ben. He had everything he needed and enough food to last him until January. A smile touched his lips.

Snowed in for Christmas.

He liked the sound of that.

Not that anyone could tell it was Christmas by the look of Ben or his house. He hadn't put up decorations for the last five years and the Christmas jumper his sister had sent him last year was hanging in the wardrobe, unworn.

As he walked back down the stairs, he turned up the thermostat. Content, he returned to his desk and his work to find a message from Darren blinking on the screen.

Just heard about the snow your way. You all right?

Ben smiled and sipped his coffee before writing a reply.

Great! Don't worry about me. Looks like I'm being

snowed in but I've got the heating on and lots of food. Everything all right with you?

One biscuit was eaten by the time Darren responded.

We only have light snow, but Cara is panicking. Scared she'll go into labour and we won't be able to get to the hospital.

Ben frowned.

Sounds rough. Anything I can do to help? Surely an ambulance will still be able to get to you. You're on a main road, right?

He checked his emails while he waited for Darren's reply.

Yup. On a main road. Snow's only just started settling, I think. We'll be fine. She's worried about everything.

Ben gave a grunt around a mouthful of biscuit.

That's understandable. Send her my love. Remember to call the baby Ben.

He checked an email from a client as Darren typed his reply.

Ha! I asked Cara about that. She actually said she'd think about it. Good for you having a nice name.

Ben chuckled to himself.

It has its perks. Good luck, mate.

He typed out a reply to his client, wishing him a happy Christmas, and then flicked back to his conversation with Darren.

You too. When are you finishing for Christmas? My last day today.

Ben typed out a reply, giving a shiver as the wind blew cold air through a gap around the old window.

I'm working through. Everyone's taking the week off, at least, so it's quiet enough to catch up on some stuff.

Ben picked up his coffee and warmed his hands around the mug.

Is 'some stuff' applying for other jobs?

Ben laughed.

Shh! They'll hear you! And no. I still don't know what I would apply for.

He sipped his drink.

Let's go into business together!

Ben shook his head.

Because that's what a sleep deprived new father needs. A fledgling business to grow.

There was a pause before Darren's reply.

Good point. Well made. Don't work over Christmas, mate. Take time off. I'll speak to you in January.

Ben put down his coffee.

See you next year.

The silence that descended over the house as the conversation ended was unnerving, despite the fact that there had been no voices, just the tapping of his fingers against the keys.

He was alone.

Alone for the whole of Christmas. A whole week to himself and no one to bother him.

Ben closed his eyes and breathed in the warming

air of his office, the scent of coffee and old books from his university days on a nearby bookshelf, and behind it all, the chill of the snow outside.

That was why it was so quiet. It was the silence of the snow blanket that was covering his part of the world.

Ben leaned back in his chair.

He could get used to this.

There came a knock at the door and Ben jumped up, eyes wide. Had he imagined that? Waiting for his heart to stop pounding, he listened carefully.

Just as he had decided he was hearing things among the muffled silence, there came another knock, louder this time.

Surely there couldn't be someone at the door. He was supposed to be alone and the snow would stop anyone getting to him. Tentatively, Ben made his way through the house to the front door, pausing on his way to glance out of a window to the porch.

There was someone there.

A woman.

He checked around, leaning against the window to see better. There was no car, no other person. Frowning, Ben opened the door.

The woman froze while reaching up to the antique bell that hung to the side of the door. It had come with the house and, as far as Ben knew, had never been used. Slowly, she lowered her arm, water dripping from her dark hair, hanging off the end of her nose.

Ben narrowed his eyes.

'Can I help you?' he asked.

The woman licked her lips and glanced back up at the bell.

'Erm, yes, please. Thank you. I'm Anna.' She pointed back towards the road. 'I've broken down and there's no phone reception and, you know, it's snowing.'

Ben looked past her to the snow and she followed his gaze until they were both staring out at the heavy falling snow for no reason.

'I don't suppose you have reception? Or a landline I could borrow? Or know where I can get some reception? Or something?'

She was rambling, but Ben couldn't blame her. It was so cold with the door open and he could practically feel the heat he was paying for rushing out to freedom.

He checked behind her again and then gave a single nod.

'I have a landline. You can get reception here, but the snow might be causing issues. The phone is there.' He pointed to a table in the hallway. 'I assume it still works. I haven't used it in years but the bill gets paid.' He stepped aside to let her in and then closed the door behind her to keep what remained of the warmth in.

She stood hesitantly on his doormat for longer than he would deem polite, until he realised she was dripping.

'Thank you so much.' Her voice came out muffled as she rubbed her reddening nose. 'It's freezing out there. It's so lovely in here. My face is defrosting.'

'Hmm. Along with your clothes,' said Ben. 'Hang on.' He rushed to the laundry room down the hallway and came back with some old towels, which he placed on the floor around her.

'Sorry,' said Anna. She removed her coat and boots, revealing a bright red and green Christmas jumper, and left them dripping on the towels before padding her way over to the phone. 'I won't be a moment. Thank you so much.'

'I didn't see a car,' said Ben, studying the wet clothes she'd left.

'No. I'm a bit further down the road. I tried your neighbour first, but no one answered.'

'They're away for Christmas,' Ben mumbled, wishing he'd thought of not answering. But what with the snow, he could hardly leave someone outside his door to potentially freeze.

'Of course. I thought they'd be home with all the lights, but now I think about it, none of them were on.' She'd pulled out her phone and was pressing the keys on the landline phone, copying the number on her screen. She held the handset to her ear and waited. 'Ages since I used one of these,' she told him quietly.

Ben blinked at her.

'Oh, hello, yes, I've broken down. In the snow.

And need someone to come help? Hmm-mm. Membership number? Hang on.'

Ben watched her fiddle with some cards from her pocket.

'It's here somewhere. Here! I got it.'

She dropped a pile of cards on the floor. Ben flinched and went to help, but stopped himself. Instead, he crossed his arms against his chest and waited as she gave her membership number over the phone.

'What? How did that happen? No, no. I'm on auto-renew. Well, why would I turn that off?' Anna sighed hard. 'Fine. Can I please rejoin? Look, I'm properly stuck. I'm a woman on her own, stuck on a narrow country lane with all this heavy snow. I'm going to freeze to death... What? Yes, I'm calling from a landline.' Anna gave Ben a look. 'Yes, well, there was a house nearby and... Hmm. But you don't know that the man in this house isn't a murderer.' She turned to Ben's wide eyes and mouthed, 'No offence.'

He continued to stare at her. Who or what had he let into his house?

Anna turned back to him and gave Ben an appraising look.

'I don't know,' she said. 'What does a murderer look like? Look, please, I need your help. I'm going to a cottage I've rented just up the road. If I could just get a tow...' She sighed. 'Fine. Thank you. Whatever.'

Ben watched in horror as Anna hung up.

'How did it go?' he asked quietly.

Anna took a couple of steadying breaths.

'Well, it turns out I'm no longer a member, but they can reinstate me. However, they're really busy right now what with the weather. With "real emergencies".' Anna did the air quotes and rolled her eyes. 'Rescuing lone women trapped in the snow and no houses nearby, I guess.' She sighed again. 'They can come out but they don't know when, they'll let me know.' Anna rubbed her hands together. 'What am I going to do? Do you know anyone who could tow me? Or give me a lift?'

'You don't have any family or friends you could call?' asked Ben, pulling a face.

'I do, but... I'd rather not.'

Anna lifted her blue eyes to Ben and he unwittingly softened for a moment. There was something incredible about those large eyes. Ben mentally shook himself.

'Well, I don't know anyone,' he told her. 'There's a farmer up the road, though. I guess I could hunt around for his number. He might be able to tow you.' Ben ran a hand though his hair, ruffling it, and looked around the hallway. 'Tea?'

Anna nodded emphatically.

'Yes, please. And thank you so much.'

Ben shrugged. As if he had much choice in the matter.

3

Anna

Mouth dry, heart pounding, Anna didn't mention to the man that she needed the toilet. That could come later. After the tea, most likely.

'Sorry, what's your name?' she asked, following him into a large country-style kitchen. She took a moment to process the size of it, with the rows of wooden cupboard doors, the small table off to one side with only two chairs, and the large window that gave the most spectacular view of the snow-covered garden.

'Ben.'

Anna suppressed the smile that wanted to appear. Ben was a lovely name. It suited him. Somehow it fitted his bulk, and even his woolly jumper and that frown on his face. When he turned to her, she realised she'd failed at keeping the smile away. She straightened her expression.

'Milk? Sugar?' he asked.

'Milk, please. No sugar. I prefer my sugar in cake form.'

Ben didn't respond, turning away to the kettle and fetching two mugs. Anna wandered further into the kitchen and took a seat at the table, looking at the other chair.

'Do you live with your partner?' she tried.

Ben looked back over his shoulder and spotted the second chair.

'No. But building only one Ikea chair was a bit depressing.'

Anna gave a small laugh and Ben caught her eye, that frown still playing between his eyes. She cleared her throat.

'So, you live alone?'

'Yup. And don't worry, I'm not a murderer.'

This time, Anna's laugh was a little forced and Ben's frown lightened, although he quickly turned his back on her so she couldn't see. She watched him intently.

The silence hung between them as Ben made the tea and Anna considered her options while looking around the kitchen.

'Did you say you could contact the local farmer?' she asked quietly.

Ben's shoulders heaved in a sigh.

'I'll have a go,' he said without turning around.

'Only, I don't want to be a bother. You know,

longer than I have to be,' Anna told him, glancing back to the snow outside the window.

'Makes two of us,' Ben mumbled, loud enough for Anna to hear, as he put her tea mug in front of her on the table.

She thanked him, giving him a curious look. He was still frowning.

'Are you expecting people for Christmas? Has the snow ruined your plans?'

Ben shook his head and sipped his tea, eyes darting back to the hallway.

'No. I didn't have any plans. Excuse me, I'll go try and find the farmer's number.'

Anna nodded.

'Thank you. I really appreciate it.'

She'd just brought the steaming mug to her lips when her phone beeped and she gave a small yelp, only just managing to not spill the tea. Pulling her phone from her pocket, she checked the top of the screen and saw them: reception bars. Glorious reception bars.

Now she just needed to figure out who to phone, if anyone.

The beep had been a message from her mother coming through.

Are you ok? Are you there? What's going on?

As she went to respond, another message came through.

Anna hesitated. If she called her mother now, she'd expect answers that Anna didn't have. Gripping her phone, Anna left the tea on the table and wandered back to the hallway in search of Ben. She found him on the landline, making agreeable noises.

They locked eyes for a moment and then Ben looked quickly away.

'Hmm-mm. Yeah, no, I understand. No problem. Thanks.'

Something collapsed inside Anna.

'Not good news, then,' she murmured as Ben hung up.

'No. Apparently he can't plough the snow or give you a tow until the snow's stopped, or at least lessened. He might be able to tomorrow. If he can, he'll look to see if he can tow your car. I imagine we'll have to dig you out by then. The farmer, that is. Digging you out. Not me.'

Anna smiled when she shouldn't have and Ben's frown deepened.

'Thank you for trying,' she told him. 'I have reception!' She waved her phone.

The frown lifted and Ben smiled.

Anna's breath caught. Well, if that wasn't a very handsome smile. She'd have to try and get him to do that again.

'So, you can call for help and be on your way,' he said, taking that smile with him back to the kitchen and his mug of tea. 'That's great.'

'Yeah,' said Anna, following him, staring down at her phone.

'What's the problem?'

'No, there isn't… I'm just working out who to call. Everyone I know is down south, it's quite a drive here and, you know…' She gestured to the heavy falling snow on the other side of the kitchen window.

Ben's frown was back.

'But it's Christmas Eve tomorrow, don't you want to contact whoever you're spending Christmas with? Can't you call them?'

Anna pressed her lips together.

'Actually, I was spending Christmas by myself.'

Ben stared at her.

'For the first time,' she told him lightly. 'It was supposed to be this wonderful big thing I was doing for myself. This certainly wasn't part of the plan, I assure you.'

'Where are you staying?' Ben asked, sitting at the table, his eyes hard and distant. Anna could practically see the cogs in his brain whirring.

'A cottage on the other side of the village,' she told him, sitting opposite.

'Call the owners, they can help?' he suggested.

Anna's stomach turned and she shook her head.

'I would, but they've gone abroad for Christmas.

Told me where to get the keys...'

'Then call whoever has the keys.'

'Oh. Yes. Okay.' She opened her phone and started going through her emails, searching for the contact. 'Here. I have a number. I'll give him a ring.'

When Ben didn't move, Anna called the number and then ventured into the hallway, as that seemed to be the place for making phone calls.

It rang for long enough that Anna almost gave up. And then, 'Hello?'

'Oh, hello. Is this Mr Cuthbert?'

'Yes, speaking.'

'Hi. This is Anna. I'm renting Ivy Cottage over Christmas.'

'Oh yes, due to arrive today, aren't you? I imagine you're not coming now.'

'Ha. Yeah. Well, I'm sort of nearly at the cottage, but the thing is my car's broken down.'

'...Right.'

'And of course, there's the snow.'

'Yes.'

'And the breakdown service can't come out, not anytime soon.'

'Ah.'

'And apparently the nearest farmer can't help while it's still snowing.'

'...Where are you?'

'Erm...' Anna looked around the hallway blankly. 'Hang on.' She dipped back into the kitchen and whispered, 'What's this address?'

'The Old Vicarage, Church Lane,' Ben told her. 'Lower Damwell.'

Anna returned to the hallway and recited the address, looking up the walls and ceiling and wooden, ornate staircase with new eyes.

There was a slow exhale through teeth down the line.

'That's a fair bit of distance in this weather.'

'Yes,' said Anna. 'But it's further for me to go back home and there's no one from home I can call. They'll have the same journey. Hours on the motorway, which I imagine won't be moving much in this.'

Mr Cuthbert sucked on his teeth and Anna pulled a face. That wasn't a noise you wanted in your ear.

'I don't really know what to do,' she added. 'I doubt anyone could tow my car in this weather, or fix it. But if someone could give me a lift to the cottage, that would be great. I'm expecting a food delivery there soon, and I only have a couple of bags.' She was aware that her voice was edging over into desperate pleading, but that seemed to be the stage she was in now. Desperate pleading might be necessary.

'I'm sorry, love. I can't get there. Not with all this snow and the weather the way it is. But you're not stuck outside, you're in the Old Vicarage? Who lives there now? Used to be Mr Wilmslow, but he died a while back. Can't remember what happened to the old place. I know it was never put on the market.'

'Erm, a man lives here,' said Anna quietly. 'His name is Ben?'

'Oh. Can you put him on?'

Anna hesitated, looking at her phone and then the kitchen door, then she went back to Ben and offered him the phone.

'He wants to talk to you.'

Ben's eyes widened and Anna didn't blame him.

He took the phone.

'Hello? Yes, this is Ben. Yes, Ben Wilmslow... He was my uncle. Thank you. It was a while ago.' His eyes darted up to Anna's and, wondering what to do with her hands, she resorted to hugging herself. Ben sighed. 'Yes. Sure. No problem. No, no, it's okay. Sure. Thanks.' He handed the phone back to Anna with great resignation, sitting back at the table and staring down into his tea.

Anna gently took the phone and ventured back into the hallway.

'Hello? It's Anna again.'

'He's old Mr Wilmslow's nephew! You learn something new every day, don't you. I'm sorry, love, but no one's going to be able to get you to the cottage today. I'd cancel that food delivery if you can, but if not, let me know and I'll try and let them in. In the meantime, Ben has agreed you can stay there. Just for the night. Is that okay?'

Anna's mouth went dry and she held on to the wall for balance.

'Erm...'

'Do you not feel safe there?' Mr Cuthbert whispered, as if Ben would hear him.

'No, I mean, yes, I do. It's not that. It's just...' She marched to the far end of the hallway and cowered by the cold front door to whisper, 'I don't think he wants me here.'

'Well, I doubt you want to be there, either. So, you're equal. Or something. Sorry. I know it's tricky. But it's just one night. Call me if you feel unsafe and we'll sort something else out, all right? And let me know about that food delivery. We'll see what the weather's like tomorrow and I'll try to come get you if you can't get the car fixed.'

Anna clenched her eyes shut.

'Okay. Thank you. I really appreciate you doing all you can. I'll let you know about the food delivery.'

She said goodbye and hung up before messaging her mother, just to tell her she was okay and that she'd call her in a bit. Then, with bated breath, she returned to the kitchen and Ben.

He didn't look up at her.

'I'm sorry,' she said, falling into her chair. 'I really didn't want any of this. If I could fix it, I would. I promise. Are you sure it's okay if I stay the night?'

Ben shrugged.

'Why not. It's a big house, there's plenty of room.'

'I don't want to cramp your style,' Anna assured him. 'You can carry on as if I'm not here.'

Ben fiddled with his mug.

'I was only going to work.'

Anna brightened a little.

'At Christmas? What do you do?'

'I'm a financial advisor for a large finance corporation in London.' Ben looked up to briefly meet Anna's eyes. 'Most people hate me when I tell them that.'

Anna laughed and put a hand over her mouth as Ben jumped.

'I'm sorry. I don't hate you. I would have thought that was more for investment bankers and the like.'

A small smile touched the corners of Ben's lips.

'So, you don't work in London?' Anna ventured.

'I used to. But when my uncle died and left me this place, they offered me remote working. I still go to London every now and then.'

'Do you prefer working from home?'

Ben nodded.

'It's quieter. Usually.' He gave Anna a look and Anna's lips twisted as she tried not to laugh again. She failed and there was Ben's smile. He brushed it away quickly and took her half-finished tea.

'I'll redo this,' he offered, turning his back on her.

4

Ben

Ben could blame the warmth in his chest on the tea, but tea had never done that before. Perhaps it was the effect of tea when it was snowing so hard outside. The blanket of white lent a new feeling to the world, even inside the house. It certainly couldn't be anything to do with Anna and her big, beautiful eyes, or the fact that she would have to spend the night. That thought sent flutters through his stomach. He'd have to make up a bed for her, preferably on the other side of the house to his own room. There was a spare bathroom on that side too, but it would need cleaning. He couldn't let her see the state of it. Perhaps he could offer a distraction while he got it all cleaned and sorted.

There came a beep and Ben looked over his shoulder to watch Anna check her phone. He frowned as her smile fell. She placed the phone down with trembling fingers and took a deep breath.

'Everything all right?' Ben asked, turning back to place the fresh mug of tea in front of her.

'Yeah. Just my stupid ex messaging me. I thought it was my mum. She's worried about me. I'm going to need to give her a call in a bit.'

Ben nodded. Great, that would be the perfect distraction. Anna thanked him for the tea and then glanced back to her phone.

'Recent breakup?' Ben asked before he could stop himself.

Anna shrugged.

'Not really. We broke up months ago because I caught him with someone else. Then they were together and I was heartbroken. Now I'm finally over him, he's broken up with her and wants me back. Ha! He can forget that.'

Ben watched her fingers as they tapped against the mug.

'That's rough. And you're over him?'

Anna caught his eye and a rush of warmth went through him. He looked down at the table and discovered his own mug empty, so he couldn't blame this warmth on his drink.

'Well, I was. I mean, I am. I definitely don't want him back, so what does it matter.'

Ben gave this some thought.

'I imagine it's a natural reaction, when someone

gets back in touch like that,' he offered. Not that he would know.

'Probably,' Anna conceded. 'Anyway, it doesn't matter.'

'What does his text say?'

'Just wants to meet up. Well, that can't happen, can it.' Anna grinned suddenly, looking towards the window. Ben meant to follow her gaze but instead found himself staring at her beaming smile, his mouth wanting to mirror her.

'Is that why you wanted to get away?' The words came out of his mouth before he had time to question them. He pressed his lips shut to stop any more falling out.

Anna looked back to him and searched his eyes in such a way that his stomach knotted itself.

'Partly. A small part, I guess. My family's quite big. My parents divorced and started new families so there's a lot of stepbrothers and sisters, and half-brothers and sisters, and more extended family. I was an only child and suddenly Christmas is this time of lots of shouting and screaming and people talking over me, whether I'm with my mum or dad. There's only so many times I can cope with being asked why I'm not married yet, when am I settling down, when am I going to start a family. And this year would be worse.'

'Why's that?' Ben asked quietly, accidentally letting his eyes graze over the woman sitting oppo-site him.

'I just lost my job,' said Anna, barely audible. She physically shook herself and stood up. 'Sorry. I'm going to go call my mum, let her know I'm alive. Is that okay?'

'Yes. It's okay that you're alive and telling your mum,' said Ben, pausing when Anna laughed. 'Why don't you go into the living room. It's comfier than the hallway. I'll be, erm, upstairs. I'll sort out a bedroom for you.'

Anna went where his finger pointed.

'Thank you.'

'No problem.' Except that it was a problem, and as soon as Anna had left the room, the problem weighed heavy on Ben. He attempted to shake it away. It was only for one night. He could do one night. She'd be gone by midday tomorrow.

Ben nodded to himself, ignoring his gut twisting at the thought, and then hesitated on the stairs at the landing window, looking out at the snow. It still hadn't stopped.

If it carried on this way, she might be stuck here for longer.

Ben didn't dwell on the thoughts that followed. He simply reached the landing, found some clean bedding and went to the bedroom furthest from his that still contained a bed. It was a guest room, mostly made up for when his parents or sister decided to visit, which they hadn't done for a long time. He gave the room a quick dust before he made the bed and finished by vacuuming the carpet. It could have done with the window open for a while, but he didn't want to let the snow in and the warm air out. He ventured into the bathroom two doors down and gave it a quick scrub before finding some clean towels, which he left on Anna's bed.

When he finished, he checked his work and smiled to himself, just as the sound of his name reached him.

'Ben?'

He trotted down the stairs to find Anna in the hallway.

'Everything all right?'

She nodded, smiling when she caught sight of him.

'Yeah. You were gone a while. I know this is a big place, but I was worried you'd fallen into Narnia.'

'I think Narnia's out there.' Ben gestured to outside and Anna laughed.

For a moment, they stared at each other, until Ben didn't know what to do with his hands and Anna looked away, clearing her throat.

'Erm, I've got food in the car. I should go bring it in. Although, I guess it's in its own little freezer out there.'

'What about your food delivery? I heard you telling that cottage bloke about it.'

Anna waved Ben's words away.

'I got a message just now. It's been cancelled because of the weather. Which is good of them, right? Still, I got a full refund, so that's something.

I've told Mr Cuthbert.'

Ben nodded.

'What food is in your car?'

'Oh, erm, there's a little turkey and vegetables, mince pies, Christmas pudding, chocolate cake, nuts, tangerines, that sort of thing.'

Ben stared at her and then huffed in disbelief.

'What was the food delivery for, then?'

'Oh, I have the worst luck,' said Anna, gesturing to her current situation. 'As you can see. I knew something would happen, I just didn't know what. And I didn't think it would be this bad, if I'm honest. Still, could be worse.' She flicked her gaze up to his and gave a nervous laugh. 'So I brought a mini Christmas dinner with me in the car, just in case.'

'Just in case you got stuck in the snow on the motorway and started a fire on the tarmac to cook a turkey?' said Ben.

'And roast potatoes, yes. What's your point?' Anna grinned playfully and Ben's insides twisted again.

He reached for his coat to cover up the feeling.

'Let's go bring in your food. I don't want you getting to your cottage tomorrow with nothing to eat because it's all spoiled. Better safe than sorry.'

He opened the front door to a burst of cold wind and a small flurry of thick snowflakes.

'You were saying?' said Anna, hugging herself against the cold. 'Hang on.' She reached for her own, still wet coat and pulled on her damp boots, pulling a face as she did.

'You have your own bathroom upstairs with a working shower, and I put towels on your bed,' said Ben, watching her expression.

Anna's face lit up.

'Oh, thank you.'

She walked out in front of him, straight into the heavy snow, and Ben watched her for a moment, wishing his heart rate would calm down. When more snow was blown into the house, Ben made a hasty exit and followed Anna down his drive to the road.

It took two trips, but finally they closed the front door, stripped off their wet coats and boots, and fell into the kitchen with the bags, breathing hard.

'I suppose if we lived in a country that regularly got this kind of snow, we'd have snow shoes, or something. And thicker coats. And many layers under those coats,' Anna said, catching her breath.

Ben laughed and then snapped his mouth shut.

'Yup.'

He couldn't help but see the curious look Anna gave him.

'I've got some space in the freezer and fridge. I can unpack what needs unpacking while you go dry off and warm up. I'll get a fire going too,' he told her.

'Don't be ridiculous. I shouldn't even be here. Let me pull my weight.'

They unpacked together, Ben instructing Anna where to put everything and Anna offering Ben a mince pie. He took it hungrily, filled his mouth with a big bite and left the remains on the side so he could show her upstairs.

'Here's your room.'

Anna was staring in awe around the house.

'This place is amazing,' she breathed. 'Oh, this is perfect. Thank you.' She stepped into the bedroom, grinning, pausing to check out the view from the window. It was mainly white.

'Where's your room?'

'The other side of the house. So don't worry, we won't bump into each other or anything.'

'But you can hear me if I scream?' Anna asked.

Ben hesitated and Anna laughed.

'This house is so old. Is it haunted?' She ran her fingers over the windowsill.

'Not that I'm aware of,' said Ben, glad he'd dusted. 'Here's the bathroom, it's just two doors down and it's all yours.'

'Thank you,' Anna repeated, following him. 'What are these other doors?'

'Bedrooms.'

Anna's eyes widened.

'How many bedrooms does this place have?'

'Six. Mine is down the hall and I have an en suite so these five bedrooms share this bathroom, but as it's just the two of us...'

Anna was staring at him with such soft eyes that

Ben found his words trailing off. He cleared his throat.

'Anyway, the towels are on your bed. I think I said that. Shall I show you how the shower works?'

'Please.'

Ben did so, with a rigid back, blinking furiously as his brain urged him to get out of the bathroom and leave her to it as quickly as possible and his body suggested he do the exact opposite.

'I don't think the house can take two showers at once, so you go first and I'll go get a fire started in the living room. Come down when you're ready.'

Anna nodded and thanked him yet again. Ben left quickly, jogging down the stairs and catching sight of the remains of the mince pie on the worktop where he'd left it. He finished it as he went to start the fire, hearing the water heater kick in and the shower upstairs turn on.

5

Anna

If she closed her eyes, Anna could imagine she was in the cosy cottage she'd booked. Hot water fell over her body, shooing away the last of the cold and easing her muscles. Her mother had panicked when she'd explained the situation and had offered to drive up immediately. It had taken Anna and her stepfather to talk her mother down. No one should be driving in this weather.

Anna sighed. She never should have left. If she'd stayed home, she'd be warm and snug on her sofa right now, ready for Christmas with two half-brothers screaming and shouting, whether they were happily playing or arguing, and her mother constantly asking Anna when was she going to settle down and did she want setting up with a friend's son? No, no she didn't.

Compared to where she could be, the hot shower in the Old Vicarage was bliss. The building was fascinating. She doubted Ben had done much to it, in which case his uncle had done a wonderful job of preserving all of the period features. She'd have to ask Ben more about the history of the place that evening. At least it would give them something to talk about.

Yes, a relaxing evening in the company of an attractive stranger for just one night wouldn't be so bad. Then, this time tomorrow, she'd be in the cottage and setting up for her first proper Christmas that would be done her way.

Her mind drifted back to Ben, the attractive stranger. Just one night, in this glorious old house, their bedrooms on opposite ends of the hallway. Anna bit her lip. There was always a possibility that this night could go better than she'd hoped. Laughing, she shook the water from her eyes and the thought from her head.

Even if she really wanted to, she couldn't see Ben going for a night of passionate sex with the woman who was gate-crashing his evening. He probably frowned during sex, anyway.

Anna laughed again and washed the last of the suds from her skin.

The huge bath sheet towel Ben had given her was so soft she wondered if it was brand new. It left fluff behind on her damp body, which suggested it was.

Dressed in dry clothes, her wet hair squeezed of

its water, she ventured back downstairs to find Ben on his knees in front of the large open fire in the living room. She wasn't sure what took her breath away the most, the beautiful room with its period features or the man stoking the fire, his jumper sleeves rolled up to his elbows revealing dark hair on his thick arms.

Anna took a moment to appreciate him and then softly cleared her throat and looked up at the ceiling rose.

Ben turned back to her and followed her gaze.

'This is a beautiful room,' she told him, walking in.

'It was my uncle's favourite,' said Ben, dropping eye contact and standing, brushing his hands together to clean them. 'He used to sit in that armchair there with a whisky or brandy – brandy at Christmas – and read a book by the fire.'

'That sounds…magical,' breathed Anna, studying the beaten, faded armchair Ben had pointed out.

'It was different. When I was growing up, we'd watch TV or play board games. Here we were expected to talk or read.'

Anna smiled.

'Sounds like my sort of house. I always wanted to read when I was a kid. But then…' Anna trailed off. 'Sorry. You don't need to know my life story. Well, the shower is free. What time is it? I can make us something to eat, if it's not too early?'

Ben shook his head.

'You don't have to cook.'

'But I want to. To say thank you.'

Ben raised an amused eyebrow.

'Okay. But don't use your food. That's your Christmas dinner for tomorrow, in your cottage.'

Anna gave him a mock salute. Ben hesitated before shaking his head and leading her back into the kitchen where he showed her the fridge and cupboards that held most of his food.

'There's a chest freezer in the utility room with other stuff, but it's probably too late to defrost anything.'

Anna put her hands on her hips as she surveyed the contents of the cupboards.

'Is there anything specific you fancy?' she asked.

Aware of the sudden pause, she glanced back to Ben and caught him looking at her. He turned away quickly and Anna grinned to herself.

'Not really. I was going to have leftover spag bol tonight.' He shrugged. 'Make what you like.'

'Okay. Is there anything I shouldn't touch? What are you having for Christmas?'

Ben shrugged again.

'Nothing. I don't celebrate Christmas.'

Before Anna could respond, he'd vanished, up the stairs and towards his en suite. Anna watched him go and then sighed, turning back to the kitchen.

'Okay, let's do this.'

She wanted to believe – and for Ben to believe – that she was a great cook, but the truth was that Anna was fantastic at putting things in the oven and somewhat all right at making sure the timings worked.

She found sausage rolls, some cold cooked beef, pigs in blankets and fresh bread, and made a decision. Working out the oven timings, she found the cupboard with the oven trays, pots and pans, and got to work.

While she waited for things to cook, she found a chopping board and selected some salad pieces from the fridge, being careful not to take too much. Then she dutifully made sandwiches, set out plates and stood back to watch the oven.

In her own bags were bottles of wine. She opened one, found a clean glass and filled it with red wine. Slowly, she meandered back to the living room and watched the flames of the fire grow and sputter.

'Probably shouldn't have left you alone,' she told it, sipping her wine. Keeping her phone close by to keep an eye on the time, she sat on one end of the sofa and listened to the fire crackling.

This, she had to admit, was like a dream. The warmth and softness from the shower, the heat of the fire, the wood crackling, the old furniture and beautiful ornate coving above her head. The house could do with some love and a bit of a refresh, but beneath the old-fashioned pieces, it was stunning.

Six bedrooms, too. If she lived here, she'd turn it

into a bed and breakfast, offering full English breakfasts and croissants out on the patio in the summer. Every bedroom would need an en suite, though. And the spacious country kitchen would probably have to be made into a professional, steel monstrosity.

Anna sipped her wine thoughtfully.

The other option in this fantasy, of course, was marrying the handsome, frowny financial advisor and helping him to maintain the house that had been in his family for... Anna twisted her lips thoughtfully and settled on generations. Yes, the house had been in his family for generations.

She'd live here as his wife and mother to his children, and every Christmas they'd recount how they met and look for the snow blizzard, their children pressing their noses up against the windows in search of snowflakes and Santa.

Anna's smile slowly fell.

And then she could go back to her own family and tell them she'd finally settled down, that there was a husband and babies, and that they could stop constantly asking her what she was going to do with her life, all alone.

Sighing, Anna threw away the fantasy of being Ben's wife in this house. She didn't want to get married. She'd gotten this far without a man, she'd gotten this far on her own.

Looking down into her wine, she almost laughed. This far. No job, no relationship, the most excitement she had was the idea of spending Christmas alone, because spending every evening and weekend of her usual life alone wasn't enough.

Homesickness twisted in Anna's gut and she sat forward to try and dislodge it.

Both of her parents' homes would be a cacophony of noise, and if she were going there she'd be wishing she wasn't. She'd be wishing she was in an old vicarage somewhere up north, trapped with an attractive man and open fire.

So, she had to make the most of this one night.

As she shifted, the wine sloshed and a little bit fell to the carpet at her feet.

'Oh, sh—' Anna stood, careful not to spill more wine, and strode back to the kitchen. She left the wine glass on the worktop and found a cloth, wetting it under the sink. When she returned to the living room, she considered the stain. Wine was notoriously hard to get out, water probably wouldn't do it. Did Ben have any stain remover? She was about to turn back to the kitchen when there was an almighty crack and the fire spat out a glowing ember, straight onto the carpet in front of the hearth.

Anna squealed and ran to it, stamping on the ember before it could get any grand ideas. When she lifted her foot, there it was; a burn in the carpet. Surely, this happened all the time. When Anna distanced herself a little, an array of burn marks revealed themselves. Although the freshest one was the largest.

'Oh, for the love of—'

She jogged back to the kitchen and then wondered why she was in there. Nothing could get out a burn mark, and that wasn't her fault. The wine was her fault. She needed stain remover.

Her head was in the cupboard under the sink when the smoke alarm above her went off.

Anna squealed loud this time, her heart jolting with the shock, although she managed not to bang her head. Falling back out of the cupboard, she searched the ceiling for the smoke alarm, and then made a grab for the oven.

Smoke billowed out as she opened the door. Thankfully, Anna caught herself in time and reached for the oven gloves before pulling out the trays of sausage rolls and pigs in blankets. She left them on the oven top while she waved at the smoke alarm with the oven gloves. Just as she was reaching for a chair to stand on to turn it off, Ben appeared.

'What happened?'

He opened the back door, letting in an immediate gust of freezing cold air and then reached up to turn off the smoke alarm.

Breathing hard, Anna waited for the panic in her mind to settle.

'Sorry. Sorry. I spilled some wine and then the fire spat and burned your carpet and I was just looking for stain remover when the smoke alarm went off, and I don't even know how that happened. They weren't in there too long.' Anna glanced back to check the pigs in blankets, and that was when her mind finally caught up and processed that Ben was standing before her topless.

Slowly, she turned back and looked at his naked, broad chest. His jeans had been replaced with tartan pyjama bottoms and Anna wondered if there was a shirt to match. Not that she was worried too much about that.

Ben gave a shiver and moved to shut the back door.

'Sorry,' Anna murmured. 'I don't know how that all happened. Other than I'm here and that's what happens to me. Sorry.'

'Stop apologising,' said Ben.

Anna attempted to also stop staring at the hair on his chest.

'Long as the house isn't burning down. The oven is temperamental, I should have told you. You need to turn it down a bit.' Ben reached over and fiddled with the nobs on the oven. Anna stepped away and watched the muscles in his back work.

'Don't worry about the living room carpet. That thing is older than me. It's okay if it gets a burn or a stain, or whatever.'

Ben turned and caught her staring. Her eyes shot up to meet his and she swallowed hard.

'No, no,' she said. 'Do you have any stain remover? I'll have a go at the wine stain. That was my fault. And I just need to put in the sausage rolls and warm up the bread, and I think we're ready. You should...' She was going to say that he should go finish getting dressed, but she didn't want him to, so the words trailed off.

Ben looked down at himself and gave a brisk nod.

'I'll be back in a bit. Try not to set fire to anything.'

Anna gave a fake laugh as she watched him go. As soon as he was gone, she fell back onto one of the kitchen chairs. If this was how this night was going to go, she might need to throw herself into the cold snow.

6

Ben

Heart pounding, Ben closed his bedroom door and sat on the foot of his bed, taking a deep breath. Another shiver ran over him and he pulled on a shirt and his jumper, wondering what had possessed him to run down the stairs half naked.

The smoke alarm, he reminded himself. The damn smoke alarm.

Still, it wasn't like him. When there was someone in his house, even if it was his sister or mother, he would lie awake in the early hours wondering if he should be the first to get up, he would lock his en suite door, he would listen for their comings and goings.

Yet, for some reason, he'd run down the stairs to a complete stranger and forgotten to even take a shirt with him. A shirt that had been waiting on the bed and would have been easy enough to grab.

Now she had seen him topless. Not only that, he'd caught her staring. Ben looked at himself in the mirror and tried to work out what kind of stare it had been. His body responded to the memory of Anna's large eyes grazing over his chest, his brain putting together the sensory components of her pressing her warm cheek against his skin, of her fingers brushing over him. He could feel her, smell her...

Ben shook himself.

'What the hell are you doing?' he asked himself quietly. 'It's one night. She's a woman on her own. You have to make her feel safe. That's your only job. Shelter and safety. Get a grip.'

He remained staring at his reflection for a moment too long, enough for him to realise just how much time had passed since he'd reacted this way around a woman. It was years, not months.

Taking a deep breath, Ben walked down the stairs and checked the living room. The fire was behaving itself and the room was empty. By the sofa, there was a wet smudge but no stain. Ben smiled, impressed.

He wandered into the kitchen to find the smoke had cleared, plates were ready on the worktop and Anna was pouring wine into two glasses.

'Well done on getting the stain out,' he told her.

She smiled, putting down the wine bottle.

'I don't know if you drink wine? Don't worry if

you don't.'

'I do,' he said, taking the wine glass she offered him.

'I promise not to spill again,' she said, holding up her hand, twisting her fingers.

Ben gave her a curious look.

'Is that how you make promises where you're from?'

Anna looked at her raised hand and lowered it.

'What? It's the brownie hand thingie. I do solemnly swear, I'm a brownie or girl guide, or whatever. I don't remember what we used to say.'

'That,' said Ben, 'is "live long and prosper" from Star Trek.'

Anna frowned and held up her hand again.

'No, it... Oh, it is, isn't it.' She laughed and the room brightened. 'Well, that as well. Live long and prosper,' she toasted, holding up her glass.

Ben shook his head, unable to stop his own smile, and clinked his glass against hers.

'Live long and prosper,' he murmured, sipping his wine. It wasn't bad. He moved to check the label on the bottle as Anna asked him where the cutlery drawer was. Ben showed her.

'Should we eat at the table?' she asked, and then, before he could answer, 'Oh, of course not, we should eat in the living room, by the fire.'

She moved to a plate filled with sandwiches and picked it up to take it through, then thought better of it and left her glass of wine behind.

Ben watched her go, his insides softening, before realising he should be helping. He picked up a plate filled with the slightly burnt pigs in blankets and another with cheese and crackers, and followed Anna.

She was moving the coffee table in the living room so they could sit comfortably and eat near the fire. Ben let her, going back to bring in more plates.

Finally, the small buffet was laid out on the table and Ben had brought in their drinks along with the rest of the bottle. He perched on the edge of the sofa, while Anna sat on the carpet, her legs tucked under her.

'Are you sure you wouldn't feel more comfortable on a chair?' Ben asked, pointing to the space beside him and then to a chair off to the side, in case she didn't want to sit so close to him.

Anna shook her head.

'Nah, I'm okay. I used to eat a buffet like this every Christmas Eve when I was a kid,' she said, piling her plate high. 'I know it's Christmas Eve Eve, but still, close enough. Come on. Tuck in.'

'This is a family tradition, huh?' Ben asked, taking some pigs in blankets he knew were his, and then some cheese that he'd never seen before.

'Used to be,' said Anna. 'Before my parents divorced. Back when it was just the three of us.' She smiled. 'The good old days.'

'My parents are divorced, too,' said Ben. 'But there were five of us. I have a sister and brother.'

'Oh. If you don't mind me asking, how come you got your uncle's house and they didn't?' Anna bit into a sausage roll and then waved at her mouth, sucking in air, grabbing her wine and taking a gulp.

Ben tried not to laugh, staring down at his plate instead.

'The official reason is that my brother lives in Thailand, so he had no use for it. My sister already owns a house with her wife.'

'What's the unofficial reason?' Anna asked.

Ben brushed some flakes of pastry from his fingers.

'I was my uncle's favourite.'

Anna grinned.

'Fair enough. You used to come here a lot?'

Ben nodded.

'I stayed here a while after I graduated the first time. It was nice to get away from everything. My uncle didn't think much of technology. No television, no internet until I installed it for him. The old dial up, remember that? All he had was a radio that we would listen to every morning while eating breakfast and every evening when cooking.'

Anna had slowed her chewing, watching him with soft eyes and a gentle smile.

'That sounds nice,' she said. 'But, hang on, when you graduated the first time? There's been more times?'

Ben reached for a beef sandwich.

'I have a master's degree. When I graduated with

that, I went to Thailand with my brother. I came back but he met a girl and stayed.'

'Wow. What's your master's in?'

'Economics,' said Ben, a grin spreading on his face as he watched Anna draw a blank. 'Yeah, it's boring.'

'Obviously not for you. We need people like you in the world. Numbers people. I'm rubbish with numbers.'

'What do you do?' Ben asked, finishing the sandwich in lightning speed and taking another.

Anna played with her food a little.

'My last job was in sales. But I wasn't good at it. Before that, I worked in admin, which was boring. And before that, retail, which was a specific circle of hell.'

Ben watched her.

'And now?' he asked.

Anna shifted and then gave a soft laugh.

'Boy, you were right. I'm too old to be sitting on the floor like this.' She gingerly untangled her legs and moved to the chair, taking her plate and drink with her. Ben waited, eyeing up the last beef sand- wich. 'Now, I'm between jobs. And careers. If career is what you call anything I've done,' said Anna in a soft voice.

Ben glanced up to her.

'You quit the sales?'

Anna gave a weak smile.

'I was made redundant, actually. Which, at least,

is better than being fired.'

Ben stopped chewing and sighed.

'I'm sorry. That sucks. I was made redundant from my last job. Recession,' he said with a shrug. 'If it helps, I'm in a better job now. Sort of.'

Anna gave him a proper smile.

'Well, the "sort of" clinched it.'

Ben laughed and then forced himself to stop, aware of Anna giving him a curious look.

'You don't have people round much, do you,' she murmured.

'These, erm, sandwiches are really nice,' said Ben, reaching for the last one and then offering it to her. She gestured for him to take it.

'Well, it's your beef and bread, so I think you need the credit for that.'

'I made roast beef last Sunday, as a treat.'

'Oh, special occasion?' Anna asked, taking some of the fresh bread and buttering it.

'I...got offered an interview in the second week of January.'

Anna met his eyes.

'So, you got a better job, but you're looking for even better?'

Ben nodded.

'Been there a while now, and I'm bored, I guess. I thought it was time to move on.'

Anna cocked her head to the side.

'But maybe it isn't?' she suggested.

Ben's stomach flipped and he looked back up,

searching those large eyes of hers. Had he been that transparent?

'I don't know,' he said quickly, shrugging. 'Guess I'll find out soon. Sorry. You've just lost your job, I shouldn't...'

'Brag about your interview? Nah, you're okay. I don't mind. I wish I could do numbers. Or anything that pays well, to be honest.'

'What will you do?' Ben asked after a moment's pause.

Anna sighed and looked around the room.

'I like interior design,' she murmured. 'And event planning. I'd quite like to run my own business, but I'm not sure what.'

'Interior design or event planning?' Ben suggested.

Anna gave him a smile that made his heart pound.

'I don't have the qualifications for either of those, or the experience.'

'You don't need them,' said Ben. 'It's not financial planning, is it. It's decorating a room or throwing a party. You don't need big qualifications, you just need...you.' He looked away as Anna's eyes softened. Was it his imagination or did she lean towards him? He studied the food on his plate.

'Maybe,' came her voice. 'I'll think about it. Speaking of event planning,' – she reached forward for more food, lifting from her seat and subtly moving round to sit beside him on the sofa – 'why don't you celebrate Christmas?'

Ben tried to not look at her or breathe her in. She smelt of shampoo and freshness, and he tried hard to think of other things.

'I don't know. No real reason. It's just always been disappointing. When my parents divorced, Christmas became awkward. Then my mum re-married and moved to Cyprus. My dad remarried and had another baby. Suddenly it was just me, my brother and sister. Then my sister got married and moved south and my brother stayed in Thailand. My uncle did Christmas but it wasn't much. So, when he died, I just...sort of...stopped.'

Anna sighed.

'I'm sorry,' she said. 'If you want, we could have Christmas together? You know, instead of both being alone.'

Ben looked up to meet her eyes and found her closer than he'd thought. She was smiling at him and it took him a moment to remember how to speak.

'Thanks, but you had your whole Christmas planned, and—'

'So what? I wanted to get away from my family. That's all. Mine is basically the same as your story, but instead of moving away, they both got new families and I didn't have a sibling or uncle to fall back on. I'm the babysitter and I sit their babies while they constantly ask me when I'm getting a promotion or a boyfriend or a husband or when I'll buy a house or get pregnant. I just couldn't face all the redundancy questions this year, not with all the screaming and shouting, and "why haven't you met anyone yet?" It's all too much. A quiet Christmas would be nice, alone or not.'

Ben stared at her. It would be so easy to lean forward and kiss her, she was so close. He turned away and blinked down at the food.

'We'll never eat this much,' he declared.

Anna followed his gaze.

'That's okay,' she said gently. 'I can wrap up whatever we don't eat. For later, or tomorrow, or the day after. Whenever you want.'

Ben shook his head.

'Some of this is yours.'

'It's okay. I don't mind.'

Her voice was too soft, it pulled his gaze back to hers.

7

Anna

Anna could barely breathe as Ben looked into her eyes. Part of her regretted moving to sit next to him, but a larger part was urging her to lean towards him. It wouldn't take much. If she just leaned forward a little, their lips could touch. They could kiss on the sofa, gently, slowly, for the rest of the evening. Maybe they'd make love by the fire rather than going upstairs. Anna's stomach twisted pleasurably at the thought, and then Ben moved away and the opportunity was gone.

Anna stared down at her food as the silence drifted on.

'I'm sorry,' she murmured without thinking. 'Coming into your house like this, a damsel in distress, ruining your work plans. I'll be out of your hair tomorrow.'

When Ben didn't respond, she glanced back up to find him frowning towards the fire. She glanced at the flames, in case she'd missed something. Ben's sigh brought her attention back to him.

'I didn't have plans to ruin,' he said quietly. Downing the last of his wine, he stood and began tidying plates. Anna watched for a moment.

'You don't have to do that. We can leave it out, pick at it.'

Ben hesitated.

'I have work to do,' he said.

Anna sagged back.

'Oh.'

Ben's gaze flitted up to hers and then back to the food.

'I guess I could leave it out.' He hovered for a moment and then refilled his wine glass from the bottle on the table. Anna passed her glass when he offered, and he filled it.

'What work do you have to do on the day before Christmas Eve? Surely everyone's shutting up now.'

Ben shrugged and straightened awkwardly.

'Just a bit of admin. You can stay here. Make yourself at home. Don't worry about imposing. It's fine.' He gave a nod and then walked out of the room.

Anna watched him go and then sat back into the soft sofa, sipping her wine and sighing hard through her nose. Tears burned at the back of her eyes but she wouldn't give anyone the satisfaction of letting them fall.

Had she read the situation that wrong? Or was Ben just nervous? She couldn't force anything, and of all the places to be snowed in for the night, a cosy living room in an old vicarage with a roaring fire and glass of red wine wasn't too bad.

Anna found her feet and wandered to the window, pulling back the heavy curtains and gasping a little at the sight of the heavy snow still falling.

At the back of her head, a small voice whispered that there was a good chance she wouldn't be leaving this place tomorrow. Anna pulled the curtains shut again and returned to the food, cutting off a piece of cheese and shoving it in her mouth. Searching for the remote control, she pointed it at the television and pressed the power button. She was just in the process of trying to work out what button did what and realising there must be another remote somewhere, when her phone beeped.

Sitting back, glad to have a reprieve from remote hunting, she checked her phone and then scoffed, throwing it back down on the table. It was another message from her ex, Brad.

She wasn't going to read it.

There was a drawer hidden in the coffee table, but it was empty. Anna stood and started pulling up the sofa cushions. When that didn't yield results, she huffed to herself and opened Brad's message.

Hey. You ok? You didn't reply. Let me know you're ok. Worried about you. Your mum says you're up north in the snow?

Anna gritted her teeth, collapsed back onto the sofa and called her mother.

'Anna! Are you all right? What's going on?'

'You told Brad where I was?' Anna asked, her voice louder and sharper than she'd intended.

There was a pause down the line.

'He was worried about you.'

'He's not my boyfriend anymore. We broke up ages ago! Why are you telling him where I am?'

'Well... Because you were so good together.'

'He's an idiot, Mum!' Anna was trying not to shout, she really was, but after that much wine and such a strange day, it was proving hard.

'He's not that bad.'

'He wanted me to do everything, Mum. Clean up after him, cook meals for him, be okay when he got drunk with his mates all the time. He wanted a mother, not a girlfriend. And then he cheated on me!'

'But he's worried about you.'

'Because his latest catch has worked out she's better off without him and has left him without anyone to pick up after him!'

'All right, Anna. I'm sorry, I'm sorry. I didn't tell him where you are, just that you'd gone up north for a Christmas all by yourself, away from your family.'

Anna took a slow breath.

'I'm thirty, Mum. I'm allowed to do my own thing at Christmas.'

'It's a time for family, Anna.'

'But you went and got yourself a new family!' Anna yelled. She put a hand over her mouth and looked back to the living room door. Heart pounding, she waited for Ben to show up, but the hallway remained dark and quiet.

'Anna!'

'I'm sorry, Mum.' Anna sat back. 'I didn't mean... Well, no, I did mean it. But I didn't mean to shout it.'

'What will the man you're staying with think?'

Anna blinked.

'Who cares, Mum?'

Her mother sighed into the phone; a habit that made Anna want to scream every time. Brad had the same habit. No wonder her mother liked him so much.

'Is everything all right there? You're safe?'

'Yes,' said Anna quietly, helping herself to some more bread. 'I made us some food and we ate. He's disappeared now to do some work.'

'Work?'

'Yes, Mum. He had plans to work today when this stupid woman turned up on his doorstep and got accidentally snowed into his house.' Anna stopped herself again, closing her eyes and taking a breath.

'You're not stupid. And I'm sorry. I shouldn't have told Brad anything. Honestly, he doesn't know where you are. I didn't give him the cottage details.'

'Good. Thank you. Not that I'm there, anyway. Just wish he'd stop messaging me.'

'So, tell him that. And I won't talk to him anymore.' She sighed down the phone again and Anna lifted the phone from her ear. 'I wish I could do something, I wish I could help. What can I do?'

'It's okay, Mum. I'll be out of this soon. Hell, I'll be home soon, and it'll all be over and we can go back to normal.'

The hot tears were back behind Anna's eyes as the pause stretched out.

'Are you all right?' came her mother's soft voice.

'Not really,' Anna murmured. 'I'm a screw up.' Tears pricked Anna's drying eyes and she wiped at them hurriedly.

'No, you're not.' Her mother sighed. 'Bad luck just seems to follow you sometimes, but you're not a screw up. Whatever it is, we'll discuss it when you're home. Forget about it until then, all right? Just, stay safe. Let me know if you need me, and enjoy Christmas. If you can.'

Anna looked around the room, with its complete absence of Christmas decorations.

'Thanks, Mum. You too. Speak to you later, yeah?'

'Okay. Love you.'

'Love you too.'

Anna hung up and stared at her phone as she worked on controlling the tears. Taking a breath and a swig of wine, she stood, paced the room and then remembered that she'd been searching for the remote.

Glancing at the doorway, she gave a small, defiant nod.

The lights for the hallway were easy to find, and it felt less like creeping if she wasn't wandering the hall in the dark. At the end of the hallway, near the front door, was a room to the right, which led to another smaller room, and there was Ben, sitting at his computer. Anna approached slowly. The first room was filled with minimal furniture; a table up against the wall, an old armchair, a few boxes. Anna stopped at the entrance to the second room and leaned against the doorframe.

'Wow, you have a two-screen job.'

Ben jumped and spun round, so Anna grinned at him.

'Sorry, didn't mean to scare you,' she said. 'I'm trying to work out how to put the TV on. I've found one remote but it doesn't seem to do much. I thought I was good with technology, but I'm stump-ed.'

'You think you're good with technology?' asked Ben after a beat.

Anna's pulse quickened.

'Of course.'

'You decided to drive up the country into a snowstorm and your car broke down.'

'Okay, in my defence, the weather forecast didn't mention a snowstorm, it said, and I quote, "light snow". And cars don't count.'

Ben looked at her.

'Cars aren't technology?'

'Not in that sense, no.'

Anna took great pride in watching the corners of Ben's mouth lift a little as he fought against a smile.

'Let me put the television on for you...' he said, standing.

'Don't call me that,' said Anna.

'What?'

'You were gonna say "grandma".'

'I wasn't.'

'You were. "Let me put the television on for you, Grandma." That's what you were going to say.'

'But I didn't.'

'Doesn't matter. I heard your head say it.'

Ben stopped and stared at Anna as she gave him her sweetest playful smile. Shaking his head, Ben ushered her out of his office, back into the hallway and towards the living room. He picked up the remote, pointed it at the television, pressed a button and BBC One came on.

Anna frowned and moved closer to Ben to stare at the remote.

'How did you do that?'

'This button.'

Anna's frown deepened.

'I did that! I tried that button.' Ben passed her the remote. 'Did I not press it hard enough?'

'You tell me,' said Ben. 'You're the technology wiz.'

Anna gave him a look and then panicked when he shifted as if to return to his office. As she was desperately trying to find a way to keep him in the room with her, he asked, 'Everything okay? I heard shouting.'

Anna sagged back a little.

'Oh, yeah. Sorry about that. I didn't mean to shout. My ex messaged me, let slip that my mum told him I was away for Christmas. So I rang my mum.'

'And shouted at her. I would have too,' said Ben gently, helping himself to another sausage roll.

'How's work going?' Anna asked.

Ben shrugged, chewing.

'Fancy watching a film?'

He frowned.

'A Christmas film?'

'It doesn't have to be.'

Ben gave this some thought and then nodded.

'Sure,' he said, brushing the crumbs from his hands. 'Hang on. Won't be a minute.'

Anna watched him leave the room and stood there aimlessly, holding the remote. After a moment, she sat back on the sofa and started flicking through the channels, wondering if Ben was coming back at all.

'Here!'

Anna whirled round as Ben came back. He grinned at her as she put a hand to her chest.

'Sorry, didn't mean to scare you.'

She narrowed her eyes.

'Well, now we're even,' she told him.

Ben sat beside her and took the remote, flicking through streaming services with the confidence of someone searching for something on their own television.

'I was just turning off my computer. What films do you like?'

'Whatever you like. Not horror,' Anna added quickly.

Ben found an action film and, with Anna's agreement, put it on. Anna didn't tell Ben she'd already seen it. They both sat back into the sofa, side by side, and a warm silence descended over them.

8

Ben

Thankfully, Ben had already seen this film so he didn't need to concentrate too hard. Not that he told Anna that. It was difficult to concentrate on anything with her sitting so close. He'd thought excusing himself to work had been the right thing to do, but in reality he'd sat staring at his screens blankly, listening to her getting upset on the phone and wondering if he should intervene. It had been a relief when she'd found him, giving him a reason to rejoin her in the living room.

It was still quite early and Ben had no idea what to do with the time when there was a stranger in the house. Although he'd had some ideas. There was a part of him that wished he'd kissed her when given the chance. She probably would have pulled away and he'd have made things more awkward, made her uncomfortable when she was stuck in this house with him. But what if she hadn't? What if she'd kissed him back and they'd kept kissing. He could have led her up the stairs to his bedroom, or better yet, they could have stripped their clothes right there and then, in front of the fire.

Ben startled from his thoughts as the fire spat a little ember onto the carpet. Jumping up, he put out the ember and then stoked the fire, putting on another log.

'Your poor carpet. You should put something down to protect it,' came Anna's voice behind him.

'It's okay. I'll replace it soon anyway.' Ben had been saying that since he'd inherited the house. He moved back to the sofa and sat beside Anna, perhaps a little closer than he had been before. He held his breath, wondering if she would lean in or move away, and he exhaled in a rush when she ever so slightly leaned into him.

Heart pounding, he sipped his wine and stayed still, staring at the television screen. Despite all his efforts to pay attention to the film, his mind kept straying. What was he doing? This wasn't him. This hadn't been him for so long.

Once the credits were rolling, Anna stretched her arms and stood to stretch her back.

'Good film,' she said, bending to pop a cold pig in a blanket into her mouth.

'It is,' Ben agreed, stretching his own arms while trying not to watch her. As she lifted her arms above her head, her jumper lifted with them, exposing some of her midriff. She wandered over to the window and peered around the curtains.

'I hate to be the bearer of bad news,' came her voice as Ben ate the last of the bread. 'But it's still snowing.'

'No. Can't be.' Ben joined her by the window and opened the curtains fully onto the white garden. Not that he recognised it as his garden anymore. The blanket of snow was so thick that some bushes had all but vanished. The snowflakes were still falling and, as they watched, a gust of wind blew the snow against the window. Ben and Anna both stepped backwards in unison and glanced at one another.

'Maybe it'll stop in the night and...thaw by dawn?' Anna suggested, without a hint of believing her own words.

'Stranger things have happened,' Ben murmured.

'Like this snowstorm?'

Ben nodded, turning back to the food, his stomach churning. He shouldn't have eaten that bread.

'Is it a snowstorm? What makes it a storm?' said Anna, bustling past him to tidy up.

Ben watched dumbfounded for a moment, before stepping in to help. Together, they carried the plates into the kitchen.

'The wind, I guess,' he said.

'It's not like you have thunder and lightning with a snowstorm,' Anna continued, discarding some food and wrapping up the edible remains. Ben watched, aware that this was his kitchen but not wanting to disturb this little whirlwind who was tidying it.

'You don't have to do that,' he said. 'I can tidy up.'

'I don't mind. You wouldn't have this mess if I wasn't here.'

Ben stepped back and watched her more critically.

'Did I hear you telling your mum that you were always tidying up after your boyfriend?'

Anna's tidying slowed.

'Yeah.'

'Was it ever because you didn't give him a chance?'

Ben flinched as Anna spun around to face him, those beautiful large eyes hard with anger.

'I gave him plenty of chances,' she said through gritted teeth. Then she caught herself and softened. 'Sorry. It's just... You offered, just now, to tidy up. You told me not to do it. Brad never did that. If I was here with Brad right now, he'd be in the living room watching TV. Probably asking me to bring him another beer while I'm at it. But you didn't, did you. We did this together, bringing everything in here.'

It took a second for Ben to realise that this was

another opportunity. Anna had stopped and was standing close enough that all he had to do was take a step and his arms would be around her. She was looking at the kitchen worktop, but glanced at him sideways in such a way that his insides squeezed and his feet nearly took that step.

Instead, they stood in silence.

'I don't imagine you'd make your partner do everything around the house,' murmured Anna.

Ben shook his head.

'I hope not,' he breathed.

Their eyes met again and Ben froze, desperate to take that step.

Anna turned her back on the worktop and faced him, her mouth open but no words coming out.

Ben's mouth was dry as he tried to force something witty or clever to escape him.

His stomach flipped as Anna took that step, closing the gap between them. She looked into his eyes, glancing down to his lips. Ben leaned in and then jumped away, heart jolting, as Anna's phone started ringing.

She stepped back, pulling the phone from her pocket and frowning at the number. Then she switched it off without answering.

'Guessing that wasn't the breakdown service,' said Ben, willing his breathing back to normal.

Anna shook her head.

'Brad. His ears must have been burning.' She sighed. 'I should probably just block his number.'

'Why don't you?'

Anna frowned. It didn't suit her. She turned back to the worktops and began tidying again. This time, Ben found his way in and helped her.

'I don't know. Maybe I just forget it's an option.'

There was a beat and then Ben said, 'That'll be because you're so good with technology.'

Anna laughed, much to Ben's delight, and she gave him a light smack on the arm.

He grinned and they finished tidying the kitchen before returning to the living room with cups of tea.

They sat together on the sofa as Ben flicked through the channels.

'There really is nothing on,' said Anna, lifting her legs to curl up.

'Nope.' Ben put the remote down on the table and then hesitated, his cup to his lips, as Anna turned her attention onto him. Slowly, he turned his head to face her.

'What?'

'I'm having a really nice evening,' she told him.

Ben's chest fluttered.

'Thank you,' she added. 'For taking me in and letting me stay and helping me out. And being fun.'

Ben barked a laugh.

'I don't think I'm fun.' He looked down at his drink. 'Actually, I think you're the fun one,' he murmured.

When Anna didn't respond, he glanced up to find her watching him, a sweet smile on her lips.

'I think you're more fun than you let on,' she told him gently. Her smile faded and she cocked her head to the side to study him further. 'Do you have an annoying ex?'

Ben fiddled with his cup, then took a swig of tea and placed the cup on the table.

'Don't we all?'

'One that contacts you out of the blue and messes with you?' said Anna quietly.

'No. I don't have one of those. But then, if I did, I would have blocked her number. Which is what you should do if you feel that way,' Ben told her, looking at her phone pointedly.

Anna nodded and picked it up, swiping at the screen until she found Brad's number. She hit block, showed Ben and then locked the screen.

Ben swallowed against his suddenly dry mouth and reached for his tea.

'How long were you together?' he asked, desperate to try and find a different conversation but drawing a blank. As if all other topics of conversation had dissolved into nothingness and there was only past relationships and nothing else.

'Six years.'

'Wow.' Ben looked back to Anna, his eyes wide. 'I can see why you had trouble blocking him. That's a long time.'

'Yeah. But blocking him is the right thing. I feel better already.' She grinned and looked around the room. 'What was your longest relationship?'

Ben's heart skipped, his stomach turning.

'Eighteen years.'

Slowly, Anna turned to face him with widening eyes.

'Eighteen!'

'Yeah.'

'You must have met young.'

'We did.'

'Did you get married?'

Ben nodded.

'In Thailand, actually. My parents were so angry. We had to have another ceremony when we got home.'

When Ben looked back up to Anna, he found she was paying far too much attention to her drink, her smile gone, her eyes thoughtful.

'Have you ever been married?' he asked, the heat of the tea rushing to his cheeks.

Anna shook her head.

'Me and Brad talked about it. He always said one day.' Her smile returned with a short laugh. 'Good thing he didn't propose. It would have been a lot harder to leave him. In the end, I just packed a couple of bags, got in my car and drove away.'

'What about the rest of your stuff?'

'My mum and stepdad came back with me the next day while Brad was at work and we put it all in my stepdad's van. When Brad found out, he flipped. We had a huge row, but I was already gone so all I had to do was slam the door on my way out. We were renting, thankfully, so that was easy enough to sort out. All of that was Brad's doing, of course. I wanted to get married and buy a house, start a family. He kept saying we'd do it soon. That's all he would ever say about it.'

'Sounds like you might never have had that with him,' Ben murmured.

Anna nodded.

'I don't doubt that. And, of course, he had my replacement lined up before we broke up.' Anna lifted watery eyes to Ben. 'They were engaged after a month.'

Ben frowned.

'I'm sorry.'

Anna shrugged.

'They broke up before the wedding. And what do I care? She'd be welcome to him. I certainly don't want him.' She stared down at her phone. 'It's time for a big change, you know? Christmas on my own was meant to be the start of that.'

'It still can be.'

Anna lifted her eyes to Ben's and his breath caught as she wiped the unspent tears from her eyes.

'What did you do? When your marriage ended?'

Ben laughed and bit down on his lip to stop himself.

'I wallowed in self-pity for a while,' he murmured. 'And then my uncle died. That did the trick to take my mind off it. I moved here, started working remotely and haven't looked back,' he lied.

Anna nodded and looked around the room.

'Well, don't take this the wrong way, but I hope no one has to die to help me move on.'

Ben smiled.

'Can't even throw myself into work,' Anna added. 'So, have you never put the Christmas decorations up, since you moved in?'

Ben followed her gaze to the fire and then around the room.

'Nope.'

Anna drained the last of her tea.

'It might get you more in the spirit,' she said, uncurling and stretching out her legs. 'I should probably get to bed. Sooner it's tomorrow, the sooner I can be out of your hair.'

'If the snow thaws.'

They looked at one another and Ben took a strange delight in watching her eyes searching his.

'You go,' he told her, looking away. 'I'll wait until the fire's died down.'

9
Anna

The upstairs of the Old Vicarage was silent in a deadened noise way. That would be the snow, Anna told herself before her mind could jump to ghosts. It was the thick blanket of snow covering the roof of the house and the edges of the windowpanes. There was a rattle that made Anna jump just as she reached the top of the stairs. Hand over her pounding heart, she realised it was the wind battering against the hallway window, and continued down the hall to her room.

Sleep had seemed like a good idea. Ben had stiffened during the conversation about Brad, the tension becoming a little too much when she'd asked him about his own relationship. His marriage. But now that she was upstairs, in the cooler, dark bedroom, she missed his presence. Or perhaps she just missed the warm glow of the fire.

No, it was definitely his presence. The bulk of him beside her, his low voice. When faced with a cold bedroom, she realised Ben had been a bit of warm safety in the snowstorm.

Anna smiled to herself, perching on the foot of the bed.

Ben had been safety since he'd opened his front door to her. She couldn't quite believe her luck, considering the bad luck that had gotten her here. Lifting from the bed, she went to the window and stared out at the falling snow.

She was about to whisper to the clouds to please stop, to let the snow thaw, when her insides twisted. She didn't want the snow to stop.

Sighing, she stayed there a while, watching the white flakes settle.

The cottage in the village would be like this room: cold and dark and lonely. Except, in the cottage, there wouldn't be a Ben on the other side of the door, just downstairs, waiting for the fire to die away.

Shivering, Anna drew the curtains and found her toiletries. Stepping out into the hallway, she listened for Ben but heard nothing. The television was off and there was silence. Another shiver found its way under Anna's clothes, and she paused, wondering if she'd hear him coming up the stairs. Instead, there was the noise of the fire grate being poked. Anna dived into the bathroom before Ben had a chance to turn off the lights and follow her up. What would she do if she met him on the stairs in this darkness?

There had already been so many moments when she'd wanted to kiss him, and one moment when she'd been sure they would kiss. Until Brad ruined it. Blocking his number had been the right thing. It had been a long time coming, and as she brushed her teeth, Anna contemplated why she'd blocked him as soon as Ben suggested it rather than when a friend had suggested it months ago.

When she ventured out of the bathroom, the hallway was still dark with the glow of the light coming from downstairs. Anna padded back to her room and as her door clicked closed, she heard Ben's footsteps coming up the stairs. She listened for his bedroom door closing and then turned to her bed, sighing.

Downstairs, snuggled on the sofa, with the fire and Ben's company, her eyelids had started to droop. She could have slept there and then, but now that she had a comfortable looking bed in front of her, her eyes were open and her brain was wide awake. Still, she made herself undress, slipped on an oversized t-shirt and climbed beneath the covers.

It was a double bed, so she took a moment to enjoy the feel of the clean sheets, starfishing her limbs out, before shivering and curling up into a little ball. When that didn't help, she sat up and found a pair of bed socks in her bag, pulling them over her feet.

That was better.

She lay on her back, staring up at the ceiling, waiting for her limbs to warm beneath the heavy duvet, and wondered who else had slept in this room.

Shadows and ghosts of residents past loomed in her mind, and Anna rolled onto her left, snuggling into the pillow. No, think of other things. What was Ben doing right now? Was he lying in his bed, wide awake, thinking?

Or was he already asleep?

As warmth moved down Anna's body to her toes, her eyelids started to droop again and she willed sleep to overwhelm her.

A scratching noise jolted her awake, heart thumping, stomach turning as blood rushed to her legs, ready to help her run. She gripped the covers and held her breath to listen. There it was again. A scratching, coming from the window. Anna stared at the curtains for a moment, tying to remember if there was a tree outside, close enough to touch the glass. The more she thought about it, the more she knew that there wasn't.

Sliding out of the warming bed, she hesitantly wandered to the window and attempted to peek through the curtains. Expecting to see bright red eyes staring back at her, Anna prepared to scream and then stopped.

There wasn't a tree outside, but there was ivy growing up the walls of the house. Part of the plant brushed up against the window, bent by the snow and wind, scratching at the glass. Anna watched it move for a while, only returning to her bed when the cold climbed up her legs and sent a shiver through her.

She wrapped herself up tight and closed her eyes, willing sleep to come again.

Eventually, she sighed, opened her eyes and sat up to reach for her phone. Perhaps some scrolling would help. She immediately dropped the phone on the bed. As if scrolling ever made her sleepy. What she needed was a book. Crawling out from the covers and across the bed, Anna stuck her bum in the air as she balanced precariously on the edge, searching through her bag.

'Aha!' She held her book triumphantly above her head and nearly fell off the bed. Catching herself, she scurried back under the covers, plumped up her pillow and got comfortable. Switching on the bed-side light, Anna returned to the novel she was reading about a woman who lost her job and moved to Italy to argue with a grumpy Italian olive farmer. She smiled at the mention of the farmer's biceps, her mind showing her an image of Ben's arms.

Pulled out of the story, Anna shook the image away.

'Stop it,' she warned herself, returning to the paperback.

Just as the narrator described the farmer's deep-set frown and full lips, her mind offered her the memory of Ben's frown, his arms crossed against his broad chest.

'Come on, now,' Anna whispered, turning and finding a new position to continue reading.

The heroine pulled at the farmer's shirt and for a wonderful split second, all Anna could think about was Ben's bare chest, fresh from the shower.

She sat bolt upright, put the book down and rubbed her face.

That was more than enough.

It was time to go to sleep.

'Go to sleep,' she told her body sternly, lying down and switching off the light. Anna closed her eyes and tried to focus on her breathing.

A creak from somewhere inside the house made her eyes open, her breathing quickening.

Puffing out a sigh, she rolled onto her back and groaned.

Should she just get up? And do what? Reading was obviously out of the question. And this wasn't her house. What would she be doing if she was home?

She'd go and watch TV, she realised, contemplating whether she could do the same thing here. Would Ben know? Would he hear her? She wondered if he was a light sleeper. She didn't know which floorboards creaked, but she bet he did. He'd probably worked it all out when he was young, staying with his uncle.

Anna gazed around the dark room. Had he slept in this room? She could understand why Ben hadn't done much work to the house; he was keeping his uncle's memory there. Breathing in, there was the smell of a freshly vacuumed carpet and the clean bed sheets, but underneath was the scent of dust and a hint of the cologne that Ben had been wearing.

She rolled onto her side. Why did he wear cologne when it was just him?

Her eyes closed and she breathed in deep, imagining that she was still on the sofa downstairs, the fire roaring, Ben beside her. She cuddled up to him, breathing him in as he placed an arm around her, enveloping her while they watched something stupid on the television.

Anna dreamt of snow and broken-down cars and Ben's voice. When she woke, cold and groaning, a little light was seeping out from beneath the curtains. She rolled onto her back, stretching out her legs, and looked across to the window.

That hadn't been so bad. And now it was morning.

Kicking the covers away, Anna sidled across the bed and pulled open the curtains. She sat back onto the bed when she saw the darkness of the night stretched out before her.

'What?'

Turning, Anna grabbed her phone and checked

the time. It was four in the morning.

'But...' She went back to the window and searched the outside for the source of light she'd seen. Opening and closing the curtains, she groaned when she realised the snow had stopped, the clouds had parted a little, and the full moon bounced across the blanket of snow.

Grinning at the sudden magic she was faced with, Anna peered down to the driveway below her. It wasn't a clean blanket, she realised. There, just below her window, were small paw prints. A fox, perhaps, sneaking across the garden in search of food. She hoped it was somewhere warm now, maybe with a full belly.

Anna climbed back into bed, leaving the curtains open, and watched from the comfort of her pillow as the clouds rolled over the moon, shrouding the room in darkness once more. As her eyelids drifted shut, snowflakes began to fall, and Anna imagined she could hear Ben's breathing beside her.

10

Ben

It had taken Ben a long time to get to sleep. At first, he laid in bed wondering what the morning would bring and if Anna was an early riser. Should he get up extra early and make sure there was breakfast prepared? No, this wasn't a hotel.

With any luck, she'd wake up, realise it had stopped snowing, pack her bags and be ready to go by the time he had made his way downstairs.

Ben often didn't feel himself frowning, but this time his forehead ached with it. Rubbing at it, he rolled over and considered the nearby mirror, reflecting the window and wall opposite. What would he see if he moved so he was reflected? A man being an idiot, that's what he'd see.

Deep in his gut, he knew he didn't want Anna to go. Not that he would admit that, even officially to himself. Only to that small voice at the back of his head that he often had to tell to shut up. That was the voice that told him to quit his job and do something completely different, to go travelling, to renovate the Old Vicarage, to start his own business, to kiss the beautiful woman who had turned up on his doorstep in need of help.

Ben rolled over, sighing heavily.

It didn't matter that she was beautiful. There were lots of beautiful women in the world. His wife had been beautiful, and look at how that had turned out. What mattered was that Anna needed his help, and he was going to help her and nothing else. He repeated those last three words to himself a couple of times, just to make sure they'd sunk in. Just because he thought she was attractive didn't mean she felt the same way, or that anything needed to be acted upon.

No. They'd wake up in the morning, discover the roads clear, the breakdown service would appear to tow her car and she'd be on her way. And that would be that. Ben would switch on his computer and get back to work, filing old projects and doing small admin jobs that he could never find the time to do when the rest of the world was also working. He would drink coffee and work until the end of the day, when he would make some food and sit in front of the fire and television. Alone.

Ben rolled over again, huffing to himself.

Was Anna asleep? He always found it tricky to

sleep in a bed that wasn't his own. Did she have the same problem?

He closed his eyes and willed sleep to come, and when it didn't, he climbed out of bed, pulled on a jumper and trousers and made his way silently down the stairs. He knew each creaky floorboard and was practised in the art of creeping about the house without making a noise. A builder had once told him that he could get those creaky floorboards fixed, but Ben was determined to never do such a thing. Each footstep reminded him of a full house, with his parents and siblings sleeping soundly as Ben tried to creep past his uncle's bedroom. Sometimes he'd make it down the stairs only to find his uncle snoring, laid out on the sofa. On those occasions, Ben had ventured out into the garden and laid on the grass to look up at the stars. A few times, his uncle had woken and joined him.

No, Ben wouldn't be fixing the creaky floorboards.

He glanced out of the window as he went down the stairs, at the thick snow still falling, and wondered what he would do if Anna was forced to stay.

Retrieving his laptop, Ben made it back to his bed, sparing a glance for Anna's closed bedroom door and listening for a moment, imagining he could hear her deep breathing, before he spent the next couple of hours sitting in bed, working.

He woke, as usual, a couple of minutes before his

alarm went off, dozed until the alarm started, groggily turned it off and stared at the time. Six in the morning, on Christmas Eve. Ben enjoyed the warmth of his bed a little longer and then swung his legs out and stood, shivering at the sudden cold. He moved into his en suite and started to get ready for the day.

Just before he left his bedroom, he opened his curtains and swore out loud.

It was still snowing, although not as heavy as the day before, and the thick blanket of white still covered the world.

Running a hand down his clean-shaven face, Ben wandered out of his bedroom and quietly made his way downstairs. He'd let Anna sleep in. There didn't seem much point in waking her.

By the time Anna made her way down the stairs, Ben had drunk a cup of coffee and was contemplating whether to make her breakfast. She appeared in the kitchen, rubbing her arms, blinking sleepily.

'Good morning,' he said, waving a coffee mug at her. 'Coffee?'

Anna nodded.

'Please. How long have you been up?'

'I get up at six.'

Anna stared at him and then reached for one of the kitchen chairs.

'On Christmas Eve?'

Ben shrugged.

'It's just another day.'

Anna laughed and shook her head.

'I suppose. Until the evening. That's when it gets really magical.' She sat at the table and watched him make the coffee.

'Why's that?' Ben placed the coffee mug in front of her.

'Santa comes!'

Ben and Anna stared at one another for a moment as he tried to work out how serious she was being. She laughed and picked up her coffee, taking a sip. 'Ooh, ouch. Burnt my tongue.'

Ben rolled his eyes, smiling to himself.

'Would you like something to eat?'

'I brought croithants,' said Anna.

'What?'

Anna grinned.

'Croissants,' she said deliberately before poking the tip of her tongue gingerly with a finger. 'For Christmas Eve and Christmas Day breakfasts. Hang on.' She stood and went rummaging through one of the bags she'd left unpacked on the kitchen work-top, raising her arm triumphantly holding a pack of butter croissants.

Ben switched on the oven and Anna laid the croissants out on a baking tray.

'The rest are for tomorrow,' she told him. 'Do you have jam?'

'Erm...'

'It's okay, I brought some. Is strawberry all

right?'

'Yes?' said Ben, watching Anna fuss about his kitchen and trying to tell himself that the warmth spreading in his chest was from the coffee this time.

'Good.' Anna pulled a jar of strawberry jam from the bag and put it on the kitchen table. The croissants went into the oven and Anna instructed Ben to fetch two plates.

'I usually just have porridge,' he told her quietly.

'But it's Christmas Eve.'

'So you keep saying.'

Anna gave him a look and then smiled.

'C'mon, humour me.'

Ben grinned before he could stop himself and sat at the kitchen table with his coffee.

'What do you usually have?'

Anna leant against the worktop as she waited for the oven to do its thing.

'I don't know. It depends on the day. And how late I am.'

Ben raised an eyebrow.

'Are you often late?'

'To be fair, it's never my fault,' Anna told him. 'There's just always...something.'

'Something?' Ben caught himself gazing over Anna's body, hidden beneath a baggy hoody and jeans.

'Yeah, like, the other day I was late for an appointment because the curtain rail fell off the wall.' She sipped her coffee. 'And another time, a pipe burst as I was eating my breakfast. And then there was the time my car was in the garage being repaired so I had to get the bus, but they moved the bus stop to a temporary one and I didn't realise. By the time I found it, I'd missed the bus. Obviously.'

'Obviously,' Ben murmured, peering at her over the rim of his mug.

'One time I couldn't find one of my shoes.' Anna frowned at that one. 'Still haven't found it.'

'What do you mean?' Ben asked, wondering at the state of Anna's home. 'Burst pipes and missing shoes, huh?'

Anna nodded.

'I know what you're thinking. My flat isn't a state, thank you very much. The pipe was fixed, and all the damage. And I keep a very tidy home. I have no idea where my shoe went.' She sipped her coffee. 'The other one misses it, though.'

Ben laughed and his heart squeezed as Anna lifted her eyes to meet his, a playful smile dancing across her lips.

'All right, so some of the things are my own doing. Because I wasn't organised enough, or because I was clumsy, or whatever. But some of it – most of it – is just the universe sticking its middle finger up at me.'

'Certainly sounds it.'

'How else do you explain the snow,' Anna continued. 'I checked the weather forecast and the roads before I left. Light snow, it said, just around the time I would reach the cottage. So what the hell is all this about.' She gestured to the kitchen window, showing the snow still falling. They both watched for a moment and then Anna sighed heavily.

'I'm so sorry,' she murmured. 'You might be stuck with me a bit longer.'

'That's okay,' said Ben softly as Anna pulled on oven gloves and went in to retrieve the croissants. She'd timed it perfectly and they came out warm and fluffy. Ben let his cool for a while before ripping it open. Anna, on the other hand, dug straight in and inhaled sharply, rubbing the burnt tips of her fingers together and reaching for the jam.

'I'll see what I can do about getting out of your hair,' she continued, sucking jam and flakes of croissant from her fingers. 'It isn't as heavy as it was, at least.'

'No, but I don't imagine anyone will be able to get out here to your car,' said Ben, trying to focus on his own breakfast. 'Don't worry about it. How did you sleep?'

'Good,' said Anna. 'You?'

Ben gave her an appraising look.

'I don't usually sleep well in strange beds,' he told her. 'So if there's anything I can do to help tonight – if you're still here tonight – then let me know. I mean anything like a hot drink or some-thing,' he added quickly. 'You know, extra blanket. That sort of stuff.'

The glint in Anna's eye as she smiled at him in that moment was enough to make Ben look quickly away, blood rushing to his cheeks.

'Thanks, but I was all right. Warm enough.' She bit into her croissant. 'I'll call the breakdown service again. See what they say.'

Ben nodded and refused to let any more words out until he'd given his inner voice a stern talking to.

11

Anna

'You're right,' Anna called through the house. Ben appeared in the kitchen doorway, his sleeves rolled up and a tea towel in one hand. Anna hesitated at the sight, tearing her eyes from the dark hair on his forearms. 'Erm, breakdown still can't come out. Not in this weather and while I'm safely tucked away in this house. Might have to go sit in the snow for them to take me seriously.' She attempted a laugh and finally managed to focus her eyes on his. 'Mr Cuthbert messaged me too. Same story. He's asking if I can stay here another night or if we should be making some snowshoes.'

'That's okay. You can stay for as long as you need to.'

There was a pause as Anna watched something flitter across Ben's face; shock, she realised, that he'd not only said those words but that perhaps he even meant them.

'Thank you. I don't even know how you begin to make snowshoes,' she said. 'I really appreciate it. I promise, I'll be out of your way soon, though.'

Ben shrugged.

'I'll just call my mum,' Anna finished, waving her phone. 'Let her know you're not an axe murderer who killed me in my sleep.'

They gave each other an awkward smile and then Ben ducked back into the kitchen. Anna took a trembling breath and steadied herself. Then she plastered a smile on her face and called her mother.

'Anna! Are you all right? Has the snow stopped there?'

'Hi, Mum. I'm absolutely fine. Ben has been a perfect gentleman and I slept really well, thanks. And no, it's still snowing. Although it's not as heavy. Breakdown still can't come out yet, though.'

'What? Why not?'

'Because of the snow. It's really thick. I think the road might be impassable, or whatever. Feels like we're snowed in.'

'Don't they have tractors up north? Can't they clear the road?'

'Probably, Mum. I'm sure they will as the day goes on. We're not the only people down this road stuck.'

'Sooner you're out of that house and at that cottage, the better,' said her mother.

Anna glanced back to the kitchen.

'Hmm.'

'You should never have gone in the first place. Christmas is about family.'

'Yeah.'

'Anna, are you listening to me?'

'Hmm.'

'Anna!'

'What?' Anna turned her back on the kitchen. 'Mum, honestly, I'm fine. I'm safe. Please don't worry about me.'

'But it's Christmas Eve.'

'I know. I just made Ben a Christmas Eve breakfast.'

There was a long pause, until her mother finally asked, 'Did you sleep with him?'

Anna's heart jolted.

'What? No! Of course not. Why do you say that?'

'You made him breakfast.'

'Because he's letting me stay in his house and he made up the spare bed for me, Mum,' Anna hissed, hoping Ben wouldn't hear. 'That's all.'

'But you want to.'

'Want to what?'

'Sleep with him! I can hear it in your voice.'

'Don't be ridiculous.'

'Oh, Anna, I know you. You're distracted. Just be careful. Please? And get out of there as soon as you can. In fact, when the roads have cleared later, we'll come and get you.'

'No!' Anna slapped a hand over her mouth and turned back to the kitchen. Ben appeared, a frown of concern wrinkling the space between his eyes. Anna mouthed, 'Sorry,' and lowered her voice. 'Please, Mum. You don't need to do that.'

'Because Christmas with your family is that bad?'

Anna groaned.

'You know that's not what I mean.'

'Isn't it? It's why you vanished halfway up the country, isn't it. To get away from us at Christmas.'

Anna tried to bite her tongue, she really did. But it was still sore from where she'd burnt it on the coffee.

'Well, maybe if you didn't make me babysit all the time,' she snapped.

'They're your siblings!'

'No, Mum. They're your children you had when I was grown up and gone. And I shouldn't have to look after your screaming, sticky kids just because I'm half related to them.'

There was a shocked silence.

'Anna! How...dare you.'

Anna clenched her eyes shut.

'Sorry, Mum. I'm safe. Please don't worry. Have a good Christmas.' And with that, she hung up.

Anna stared at her phone screen, replaying her own words; she'd just shouted at her mother on Christmas Eve and then hung up the phone. Her chest began to feel tight and suddenly the next breath was hard to take in.

'Oh, no, no, no.' Anna felt for somewhere to sit and ended up on the bottom step of the stairs.

'What's wrong?' Ben reappeared, his sleeves still rolled up to his elbows but the tea towel was gone. He hovered over her, wringing his hands. 'What happened?'

'I shouted at my mum and then I...hung up on her.' Anna stared down at the phone in her hand, waiting for it to ring and for her mother to unleash a new hell on her. 'I called her kids screamy and sticky.' She glanced up at Ben.

He nodded and she shifted up so he could sit beside her.

'I heard.' He glanced at her. 'I'm guessing she pushed you a bit, though?'

Anna put her head in her hands.

'I'm going to have to apologise,' she said through them. 'Even though I was right.' She sighed and dropped her hands, opening the messaging app on her phone. Ben watched over her shoulder as she typed out an apology, his bulk beside her an odd comfort. Anna reminded herself that she barely knew him and resisted the urge to lean into him. 'What do you think?' She showed him the message.

He read it and gave a singular nod.

'Having never met your mum and knowing practically nothing about the situation, I think that's good.'

Anna laughed and hit send, leaning back and

groaning.

'I'm sorry. Bringing this into your house. I'm such a screw up.'

'You're not a screw up.' Ben's voice was so soft that Anna looked round at him. 'And stop apologising.' He was saying all the right things but there was that frown, still etched into his forehead and between his eyes. It was all Anna could do not to reach out and soothe the frown away.

'Sorry,' she murmured, giving him a grin.

Ben went to stand.

'So, you're stuck here another day,' he said, awkwardly rubbing the back of his head.

'Yup. Look, just act like I'm not here. What would you normally be doing on Christmas Eve?'

Ben gave her a strange look.

'Working.'

'Right.'

'What would you normally be doing?'

Anna glanced around the hallway.

'Christmas Eve morning, I'd be getting ready to head over to my mum's. Or my dad's.'

'Your dad hasn't contacted you?'

'No. They're the ones I should have spent Christmas with this year. When I announced I wasn't coming, he booked for his family to go abroad. Mum invited me to hers instead, but I'd already booked the cottage. So, Dad's away on the trip of a lifetime.' Anna barked a laugh and then looked up at Ben. 'Although...' she murmured.

Ben's eyes lifted to hers.

'Although?' he prompted when she remained silent.

Anna shrugged.

'This isn't so bad.'

For a moment, Ben's frown lifted. Anna watched him curiously. There was something incredibly attractive about him when he frowned, but when it lifted there was something else. Something softer and warmer, and while Anna didn't mind the frown too much, she felt in that moment that she could make it her life's mission to make it lift as it had just done.

'You can go work, if you want. I'll find something to do,' she told him, waiting for the frown to return. Ah, there it was, creasing up between his eyes. She wondered if it ever gave him a headache. 'Do you have any Christmas decorations? I have some in my car. Maybe I should go out and check the road, anyway. See what it's like. Will the road be plough-ed, do you think?'

A smile flickered across Ben's lips at all the questions.

'Erm, let's see.' He flicked a finger up. 'Yes, in the loft somewhere.' He lifted a second finger. 'That's probably a good idea but I'll come with you. Might never see you again, otherwise. Lost in the snow and ice. And' – he lifted a third finger – 'probably. But not until later, I imagine. Even when it is ploughed, it'll be icy.'

Anna had cocked her head to the side.

'You're worried you might never see me again?' she asked gently.

Ben realised what he'd said and his expression fell. Anna laughed.

'It's okay. I know what you meant. Knowing me, I'll slip, fall and twist my ankle, be buried by a load of snow and die, frozen, just a step from your driveway. Can't have that.'

Ben gave a nervous laugh and then cleared his throat.

'Yeah. That's what I meant.'

'Clumsy me,' said Anna, almost testing, watching his reaction. Ben turned away to find his boots. 'Let's go check the road, get the decorations and I'll cook tonight. Yeah?' she continued.

'You can use my decorations. But we can go check the road. See if your car is still there.'

Anna pulled on her boots and coat.

'Sure. Because a big yeti might have appeared in the night and pushed my car away?'

Ben hesitated, and for a delicious moment they looked at one another. When he turned away to open the door, Anna found herself short of breath.

The car was where she'd left it, although there was decidedly more snow than she remembered. She slipped and fell through it, her feet getting wetter and colder as each step sent snow falling into her boots. Pointless things. She might as well be out there in just her socks.

'Is there anything you want from the car?' Ben asked, surveying the scene.

Anna unlocked it and went to open the door, laughing as she pulled on it.

'Nope. It's frozen shut.'

Ben's frown deepened and he waded over to her, taking her place and giving the car door a yank. It opened with a pop.

'Wow. The strength of you,' Anna told him, and watched the heat rise to his cheeks. That was dangerous, given the temperature out there in the snow, she'd rather his blood stayed near his vital organs.

She reached into the car and pulled out two of the remaining small boxes.

'Do you have a tree?' she asked over the wind that swept around them, throwing snowflakes into their faces.

'Yup. No idea what state it's in, though.'

Anna thrust the boxes into his arms and then reached back in, pulling out a long, heavy cardboard box. She immediately lost her balance and wobbled to the side. Ben caught her and suggested they swap. He took the Christmas tree box, carrying it under one arm, with another of the boxes on his other side. Anna locked her car and followed him back to the house, unable to stop staring at the bulge in his arms.

'Maybe we should see if we can get your car onto the driveway,' he called back to her. 'In case a tractor with a plough does come through.'

Anna shook her head.

'Engine's dead, remember?'

Ben nodded.

'Yeah. Right.' He opened the front door and they fell into the warmth. Ben dropped the boxes in the hallway and then ventured back to the porch to shake off the snow.

Anna did the same and they stripped out of their coats and boots, both admiring Anna's wet socks.

'I'm going to go change. Your decorations are in the loft? How do you get up there?'

'You don't. I'll go get them.' Ben herded Anna up the stairs and when she ventured to her bedroom to find dry socks, he pulled down the loft hatch.

Anna's stomach fluttered at the feeling of his presence so close to her. Like they were an old married couple, in from a walk in the snow and he was fetching the old decorations for her to make a start on before he disappeared into his office with a coffee. Anna sat on her bed and realised she was grinning to herself. She wiped away the smile, gave her reflection in the mirror a firm nod and pulled off her wet socks.

12

Ben

Anna led the way back down the stairs after a short argument over who should carry the box with the Christmas decorations. Ben had seen enough and the last thing he wanted was Anna slipping and falling down the stairs while carrying a box of glass baubles and fairy lights. Not that he told her that. He simply made her go down the stairs first and she eventually obliged. He put the box in the living room. There weren't many decorations, although the box was big and heavy. With aching arms, he left Anna to it and went into the kitchen to make a coffee.

'Want one?' he asked without thinking.

'Please!' came Anna's voice.

Ben caught himself smiling and cleared his throat, wiping a hand down his face. That was enough of that. He left her coffee on the table in the living room as she pulled out the fairy lights and tried to untangle them.

'I'd offer to help but I think you're on your own with that,' he told her, accidentally smiling again. He hesitated in a moment of fascination as Anna's cheeks flushed and she nodded, grinning happily to herself.

Holding his breath, Ben escaped to his office and switched on his computer, sipping his coffee.

An hour or so had passed, his coffee cup empty and the screen giving him the start of a headache, when the light above his head went out at the same time that he heard a squeal from somewhere in the house. Ben looked up at the light, his frown making the ache at his temple sharper. As he left the room, he tried the light switch, but flicking it on and off did nothing.

The house was dark and quiet. Ben crept through the hallway, following the sound of muffled cursing until he finally pinpointed the reason for the dead silence hanging in the background. The fridge was off. As was the freezer. The hum that hung in the background to his life was gone. His frown deepening further, Ben stopped in the doorway to the living room and leaned against the frame as he watched the back of Anna with her hands on her head, mumbling to herself.

'Why did you do that? You idiot. Now what? Hmm? Now what are you going to do? He's going to hate you. That's what. He's going to hate you and kick you out and never want to see you again.' She gave a deep sigh, turned around and froze, her eyes wide as she caught sight of Ben. He gave a small wave.

'What happened?' He lifted from the doorframe and stepped into the room, peering down at the tangle of fairy lights on the floor, then gazing up at the plastic tree in the corner of the room. Fairy lights weaved around it and baubles and tinsel took some of the plastic edge off. It still looked awful compared to a real tree, but given that it was Christmas Eve and there was a foot of snow outside, it was probably too late for the real thing.

'Well...erm...I finished the tree.' Anna gestured to the thing in the corner. 'And I went to turn the fairy lights on, and...' She sighed again. 'I'm so sorry, Ben. For all of this. Thinking that I could escape just one Christmas, ending up outside your door, pretty much nearly burning the place down, and now...' She glanced back to the tree. 'Something's blown and all the electric is off.'

Ben almost laughed but he caught himself in time.

'Don't be ridiculous,' he told her gruffly. 'Those are my lights, right? They're over twenty years old. It was bound to happen sometime.'

'But it happened with me,' Anna murmured.

Ben couldn't stop the smile he gave her.

'Of course.' He gave her a shrug, pulled out his

phone and turned on the torch. 'It's fine, though. Honest.' He left her, walking back into the hallway and opening the fuse box beneath the stairs. 'It's only the electrics downstairs,' he said, flipping them back on. 'But you'll have to take those lights off the tree and try another set. Didn't you bring some of yours? They're probably safer.'

He closed the fuse box, turned around ready to return to Anna in the living room and found her right behind him. He stopped with a shudder and an oomph, crashing into her.

'Sorry,' she murmured, looking up at him. She apologised but she didn't move. Instead, they stood far too close to one another and stared into one another's eyes.

'Stop apologising,' he told her. Again.

A smile brushed over her lips and Ben found himself leaning down towards her. He stopped, but didn't retreat, his breath quickening. Anna pushed up on tiptoes and pressed her lips gently against his. She broke the kiss immediately, dropping back to her normal height and staring at him, waiting for his reaction.

Ben was waiting too. What should he do? What did he want to do?

His body reacted first, along with an impulse to wrap his arms around her and pull her close for another kiss. Instead, he leaned back and considered her.

'Sorry,' she whispered before clapping a hand

over her mouth.

Something inside Ben gave way, his heart pounding, his fingers and legs fizzing.

'It's okay,' he said carefully. 'I just...erm...better go...upstairs.' He pushed past her and climbed the stairs alone, despite everything inside him screaming to turn back to her, to invite her up with him, to rush back and hold her. 'Just, erm, be careful with the lights,' he mumbled as she vanished from view.

Sitting on the edge of his bed, the door closed, Ben took in some deep breaths and wondered how he could have handled that differently. Had he wanted that kiss? Yes. It came as something of a shock, but yes, he wanted that kiss. If it happened again, he'd kiss her back. Maybe next time he'd manage to not run away. What was she doing now? He couldn't hear much movement downstairs. Ben clenched his eyes shut.

What was he doing?

He'd known this woman twenty-four hours, if that. Why did he keep forgetting that? She'd come to his house in need of help, the last thing she wanted was to be alone with a strange man who then kissed her.

Except that she kissed you.

Ben replayed the moment he'd turned around, ready to go looking for Anna, only to find her right there in front of him. There had been a moment and he'd leaned forward, but then he distinctively remembered catching himself and stopping. She was the one who had come forward enough to brush her lips over his.

She had kissed him.

Ben exhaled slowly and looked up at the bedroom door.

The question wasn't whether he'd done something wrong, it was whether he wanted her advances or not. Wasn't that why he'd run away? He knew he'd definitely run away. As the kiss had broken and the overwhelming urge to kiss her again had flooded through him, adrenaline had filled Ben's body, pushing him up the stairs and away. He'd have probably gone through the front door if the weather was kinder.

He rubbed his hands over his face.

Why had he run?

Ha! Ben lay back on his bed and stared up at the ceiling. That was an easy question. Ben gave this some consideration and then berated himself. Enough time had passed. A fascinating woman had just kissed him and he had run away! Ben covered his face with his hands and let out an exasperated groan. Dropping his hands, he kept his eyes closed and relived the kiss again.

And again.

Ben only became aware that he'd fallen asleep when he slowly woke up. He was still lying on his back, on his bed, staring up at the ceiling, only now his back was on fire. Moaning, he tried to roll over, managed it slowly and curled up to stretch his back a different way. The muscles eased as he rubbed his eyes and tentatively sat up, scooting to the edge of the bed. He took a deep breath and realised what had woken him. A warm, delicious smell was infiltrating the room. Rubbing the small of his back, Ben stood and checked out the window. It was dark outside. How long had he been asleep? Pulling out his phone, he checked the time. Five o'clock. He'd somehow managed to sleep most of the day. The snow falling was much lighter but everything was still blanketed in white. He could just see the road from his bedroom window, through the trees, and could tell it hadn't been ploughed. His stomach flipping, Ben opened the bedroom door and made his way downstairs. He paused at the sound of voices before realising, only when they seemed to burst into a Christmas song, that it was the radio coming from the kitchen, which was where he found Anna.

Oblivious to him, she was dancing around the worktop, stirring something in a pan and swaying her hips as she sang the words wrong, louder than the radio could manage.

Ben folded his arms and leaned against the door frame, smiling as he watched her, letting his gaze drift over her until she turned and froze mid dance move.

'Holy hell, stop doing that!' she shrieked, flicking something tomatoey at him.

Ben laughed and Anna stopped.

'Did I just make you laugh?'

Ben wiped the grin from his face.

'No. What are you throwing at me?'

Anna studied him before moving over to turn the radio on her phone down.

'I did. I just made you laugh. Which means you don't hate me, right?' She grinned and then faltered. 'I'm sorry. About earlier. I really shouldn't have done that. This is your home and you should feel safe here, and not have random women creeping up on you and kissing you. Although, to be fair, you crept up on me first, and just now again. And you lean against the door like that, like that's not really sexy. Which you know it is, because that's what men do in films and books, and you must have seen at least one of those films, so you know it is. But that doesn't excuse what I did. And I'm sorry.' Anna let out the remaining air in her lungs in a sharp exhale, looking down at the floor.

Ben raised an eyebrow.

'It's all right. I shouldn't have run away.' He followed her gaze and found the splodge of sauce she'd flicked at him on the wooden floor. 'You think I'm sexy?'

'No!'

Ben glanced up at Anna's squeak and found her cheeks flushing as she shook her head and turned back to whatever was in the pan.

'Okay. Well, don't apologise for the kiss. It's all right. I'd just saved you from an evening spent in darkness, I was a hero. And, just so you know, I enjoyed the kiss.'

Ben found a cloth and wiped up the spot of sauce on the floor. Anna slowly turned to watch him.

'You did?'

'Yeah.'

There was a pause.

'Where have you been?' she asked quietly. 'I thought about coming to find you, but then I wanted to give you space. Honestly, I would have left but—' She gestured to the window and the white snow covering the garden, reflecting the light of whatever it was out there that was giving off light. From the kitchen window, perhaps. Ben knew the stars and moon were covered by thick cloud, so it couldn't be that.

'I'm glad you didn't leave,' Ben murmured, leaving the cloth by the sink for later. 'I'm sorry I disappeared. I just went upstairs to... And I fell asleep. I never do that.' He rubbed the back of his neck.

'Must have needed it,' Anna said gently, looking at him sideways. 'Do you feel better for it?'

'If you don't count the slight headache and crippling backache, yeah.'

Anna pulled a face.

'I think you're napping wrong.'

Ben smiled.

'Well, I'm new to it. I'm sure I'll learn.'

Anna laughed.

'You missed lunch. You must be starving.' She returned to stirring.

'I am a bit. What have you been up to while I've been accidentally sleeping?' Ben peered around her to the contents of the pan.

'Oh, well. When I realised that I couldn't leave you in peace, I thought I'd make a peace offering instead. See? It's chilli. Not very Christmassy, sure. But it's warming and filling. Sort of my comfort food. I don't know what your comfort food is.' Her gaze flicked up to him.

'It smells amazing,' he murmured, wondering what he would consider comfort food.

'But before I did this, I finished putting up the decorations. I thought you should have a Christmassy house, even if I don't stay.' Anna gestured to the door and Ben followed her out of the kitchen and into the living room.

At the door, he stopped and gasped. The Christmas tree was lit up and somehow appeared less plasticky than before, strewn with tinsel and hung with baubles. More lights were draped over the mantelpiece along with the odd bauble and some plastic garland. The room was bathed in the soft glow of white fairy lights and on the coffee table was a plate of mince pies.

'Just need to light the fire,' said Anna. 'And I didn't dare do that.'

'It's lovely,' said Ben. 'It looks like when my uncle would decorate.'

'Really?'

Ben nodded, swallowing on a rising lump in his throat as the memories rushed over him. His uncle had always had a real tree, of course. You couldn't fit many presents under that plastic one. But the decorations and the lighting and the atmosphere were all the same. All that was missing was a glass of whisky for his uncle and for the fire to be lit.

'I'll light the fire now,' he said absent-mindedly, stepping into the room. Remembering himself, he turned back to Anna. 'Thank you. For this. For all of it.' He turned back to the empty fireplace, lost in thought, unaware of how Anna watched him.

13

Anna

If she closed her eyes, Anna could almost forget what a normal Christmas was for her. She certainly couldn't believe she'd only met Ben the day before. He wandered into the kitchen smelling of the first sparks of fire and brushing his hands together. She told him to wash them before he helped gather the bowls. Anna heaped rice and chilli into each one as Ben poured some wine and then they gathered everything together and headed into the living room. The fire was the finishing touch, bringing a true feeling of Christmas to the room. Anna sat on the sofa and took it in, the crackling of the flames licking the wood, the twinkling fairy lights bouncing from the tinsel and baubles. Grinning, she leaned back and sighed.

'This is what I wanted,' she murmured to herself.

'A peaceful, cosy Christmas.'

Ben sat beside her and placed a bottle of red wine on the table.

'Alone?'

'No,' she said, watching his features in the dim light. 'No. I prefer this.'

His eyes met hers and she smiled at him, her heart fluttering, wondering how he would react. He returned the smile and held up his wine glass. Sitting up and reaching forward, she picked up her own glass and they clinked them together.

'Merry Christmas Eve, Ben. My hero. You brought me in from the cold and you saved me from an evening of darkness.'

For a moment, Ben's eyes softened and then he shook his head, looking away.

'Just doing what anyone else would do.'

Anna's smile drooped a little but she quickly brushed away the comment and dug into her food. It was fair enough, they barely knew each other and she'd already implanted herself into his home and onto his lips. She buried the chuckle that rose inside and shoved more food into her mouth.

When she was about halfway through her chilli, she couldn't take it anymore.

'So, are we going to be those types of people who just pretend the kiss never happened?' she blurted, staring down at her food.

Ben shifted and she waited for him to say something. Anything.

'You don't want to be those people?' he asked carefully.

'No, I think we should talk about it, at least.'

Ben sighed.

'All right.'

Anna licked chilli from her lips and studied his profile as he filled his fork and then his mouth with food, avoiding her gaze.

'All right. I don't want things to be awkward,' she told him. 'I don't know if you noticed, but the road isn't ploughed. And tomorrow's Christmas Day. My guess is that the farmer has a family to spend the day with, and the council obviously don't care about this road. So chances are, I'm going to be stuck here at least another day. And I know I've already said this, but I'm sorry I kissed you. I never wanted to make you feel uncomfortable or like you had to get away from me.'

Ben carefully, slowly, placed his almost finished bowl of chilli on the table. Clasping his hands together, he stayed leaning forward.

'You didn't make me uncomfortable. You didn't do anything wrong. I liked the kiss. I wanted the kiss.'

'You did?'

'Me running away was nothing to do with you.'

There was a pause and Anna placed her own bowl on the table, rearranging herself so she was level with Ben but giving him space.

'Do you want to talk about it?' she offered.

Ben sighed.

'I just...don't have the best of luck with women.'

'How do you mean?'

Ben sat back on the sofa and wiped his mouth with his hand.

'Relationship-wise.'

Anna shifted her weight, trying to work out what he was struggling to say.

'Me too. I mean, you've seen the messages from my ex. He doesn't even seem to understand that he is an ex. And my mum's not helping matters.'

Ben shook his head.

'That's nothing compared to my experience.'

Anna pressed her lips together in case words she didn't mean fell out. What was she supposed to do with that?

'I'm sorry, Ben, but you can't say something like that and expect me not to ask. You don't have to tell me, we don't know each other well yet, and you should know that I'm incredibly nosey.'

Ben gave her a sideways look and she attempted a hopeful smile. Eventually he sagged back into the sofa.

'Okay. But I haven't really told anyone this in a long time.'

Anna held her mouth shut and waited.

'I'm divorced.'

'Yes,' said Anna when it appeared Ben had stopped talking. She waited for anything further, giving him a little prompt with her eyes.

'We got married young, we met at university. Eventually, we started trying to have a baby. She really wanted to start a family.'

Anna's stomach twisted. She did her best to ignore it and stayed quiet.

'But we struggled. It took a few years. We ended up having to go to the doctors, getting tests done, all that sort of thing. Everything came back clear, no one knew what the problem was.'

Anna nodded, sipping her wine.

'That must have been difficult,' she murmured.

'It was. But then she got pregnant. I was over the moon. Years of wondering if maybe becoming a dad just wasn't on the cards for me, and then finally it happened.' Ben gave his own glass of wine a sad smile. Anna's chest tightened at the sight.

'What happened?' she breathed, not really wanting to know the answer.

'Oh, don't worry. Nothing happened to the baby. She was a very healthy, happy baby.'

Anna exhaled in a rush.

'And your wife?' she asked tentatively.

'She was fine, too. Until a couple of months into family life, massively sleep deprived, she let slip that the baby wasn't mine.'

A silence descended over the room and Anna stared at Ben with wide eyes.

'What do you mean?'

Ben shrugged.

'I mean, she got frustrated that she wasn't

getting pregnant and fell into the arms of a man she worked with. The affair lasted until she was about four months pregnant when, apparently, she broke it off. Two months after our – her – daughter was born, she realised she wanted to be a family with him and not with me.'

Anna's mouth fell open.

'But... What... Why...'

'Exactly,' said Ben, downing the last of his wine and reaching for the bottle to refill. He offered to top up Anna's drink and she accepted, holding out her glass. She was still grasping for words.

'But you were the father. You'd been there for the pregnancy, you were bringing up the baby.'

Ben sagged back again.

'Hmm.' Slowly, he lifted his eyes and met Anna's gaze.

'I'm so, so sorry,' Anna murmured. 'That would have killed me.'

She jumped when Ben barked a laugh.

'I demanded a paternity test. I guess I was panicking. And then shortly after she left, my uncle died and left me this house. The paternity test proved I wasn't the father, so I packed my bags, left London and here I am.'

Anna studied Ben as he guzzled more wine, his eyes dull and there was a slight tremble in his fingers holding his glass.

'Were you tempted to stay and keep being a dad?' she asked carefully. She regretted the question instantly as Ben's eyes started to redden. He nodded ever so slightly.

'Yeah. I thought about it. About fighting harder. But every time I looked into that baby's eyes, I knew they weren't mine and they weren't my wife's. She had her dad's eyes. And I just…couldn't. It's not like me leaving meant she had a bad life. My wife made the decision, arguably later than she should have, about which family she wanted. And it wasn't me. I couldn't give her what she wanted.' He shrugged again, harder this time, and gulped more wine.

Anna pulled a face, turning to stare into the fire.

'Do you still have contact with your wife?' she asked, watching the flames.

'No. I filed for divorce. We just split everything, to get it all over with as quickly as possible. I haven't spoken to her since.'

Anna sipped her wine.

'I'm really sorry you went through that.'

'It's okay. I'm okay.'

'No wonder you ran away when I kissed you.' Anna gave Ben a sideways look. He was staring down at his drink. 'Something huge like that would leave you with…' She trailed off, searching for the right words.

'Trust issues?' Ben smiled to himself.

'And yet you let a strange woman into your house,' Anna pointed out. 'Let her stay the night and everything.'

'Well, I have trust issues, I'm not a murderer.'

Ben gestured to the falling snow on the other side of the pulled curtains.

'And I'm forever grateful,' said Anna, holding out her glass. After a moment, Ben clinked his glass against hers. 'Thank you for telling me. I know that must have been hard.'

'I just needed you to know that me running away when you kissed me wasn't…' Ben took a deep breath. 'It wasn't about you. Or the kiss. I enjoyed the kiss. I just…'

Something twisted pleasurably inside Anna.

'Don't want to be hurt again?'

Ben nodded.

'Well, no one can promise that you won't be hurt again,' Anna said gently. 'But I can promise that I will never hurt you like that. I wouldn't be able to live with myself if I'd done that to you.'

A tension grew between them and Ben lifted soft eyes to her, a smile playing on his lips. Anna willed it to grow into a full smile. What could she do or say to make him smile properly?

'But you enjoyed the kiss?' she said, leaning forward a little.

Ben cottoned on quick, his eyes widening.

'Yeah. Yeah, I did.'

'If I kiss you again, do you think you'll run away again?'

The smile on Ben's lips grew.

'No. I won't.'

Grinning, Anna moved forward and as her eyes

began to close, Ben's grip was on her wrist and he took her wine glass from her. She opened her eyes in time to see him saving the wine from sloshing over the side of the glass. Anna let Ben take the wine glass from her and sat back, sighing.

'I'm really bad at this,' she said quietly. When Ben glanced at her, she added, 'All of this.' She went to open her arms to encompass everything around her but thought better of it.

'You're not bad at anything,' said Ben, gesturing for her to sit up. She did so and he moved forward until his lips brushed against hers for a moment.

Everything stopped and Anna became acutely aware of the beating of her own heart.

'The universe is against you,' Ben murmured against her lips. 'You just need someone standing beside you.'

With a light moan, Anna leaned forward and kissed Ben hard. He wrapped his arms around her, pulling her in further.

14

Ben

They stayed that way for longer than Ben could keep track of. Leaning against the back of the sofa, his arms around Anna's waist, her fingers sliding up into his hair in such a way that he wanted to lift her and carry her upstairs. He was vaguely aware of the crackling fire and the glow of the fairy lights, of how beautiful she'd made the room, of how warm the house had become since she'd arrived. The kiss deepened, her breath quickening and somehow they moved closer, clinging to one another. Ben ran his hands over her back, down to her hips and Anna responded by moving them towards him.

The crackling of the fire vanished, leaving only the warm glow and the heat of Anna's mouth and fingers. He needed more. His fingers pulled at her clothing until he stopped himself, hesitating in the kiss. Anna didn't hesitate. Where he backed off, she moved forward, until she stopped. The kiss broke and she looked into his eyes with something akin to glassy pleasure. Ben licked his lips, trying to think calm and rational thoughts.

'Are you okay?' she breathed.

Ben nodded, not trusting himself to talk.

'You want to do this?'

He wasn't clear on what 'this' was, but it didn't matter. His answer was yes. He nodded again, happy to let her lead.

Anna leaned into him, their lips finding one another and this time the kiss was deep from the beginning. Her hands left his hair and travelled down his chest, plucking at his shirt. Ben groaned and then froze a little, not wanting to make any silly sounds. Anna smiled and broke the kiss to check on him again. He grinned and pulled her back to his lips.

Climbing onto his lap, Anna straddled him, leaving him nowhere to hide his true feelings about the situation. With her wrapped around him, Ben relaxed into the sofa, enjoying the sensation of Anna's fingers sliding beneath his jumper and t-shirt, brushing against his skin, sending shivers through him despite the heat.

The sudden sound of Anna's phone beeping made them jump apart, both breathing hard. Bewildered, Anna found her phone and frowned.

'Who is it?' Ben asked, gazing down her body to

where her top had pulled down and to the side, giving him a glimpse of what was beneath.

'I don't know.' Anna sat back on Ben, opening the message. Her eyes widened and then, growling, she showed it to Ben.

Anna, it's Brad. I can't get through. This is a mate's phone. Are you ok? I can come rescue you.

Ben looked up at Anna's eyes, narrowed with thoughtful rage.

'I guess there are ways around being blocked,' he muttered. 'What are you going to do?'

'I'll tell you what I'm going to do,' Anna said, typing out a message.

'What are you doing?' Ben sat up, moving Anna on his lap so he could see the screen.

That's because I blocked you, Brad. I'm fine. Please leave me alone.

She hit send and then blocked the number. Trying hard not to smile to himself, Ben waited for Anna to make the next move. When she didn't speak, he studied her face, still angry and thought-ful.

'Are you okay?'

She nodded.

'I'm sorry that interrupted us. I just don't know how I'm going to get rid of him.' She put the phone on the coffee table and turned to Ben, pushing him against the back of the sofa. 'Do you want to forget that happened?' she asked, her voice quieter, a little timid, although she only stopped leaning into him once their noses were touching.

'Definitely,' Ben breathed, catching her lips in his.

Anna kneeled, lifting herself until her face was above his. Ben's hands automatically moved to her rear, stroking the shape of her, squeezing as she kissed him hungrily. Her fingers were under his jumper and shirt again, brushing against his stomach. She was moving too slowly. Again, he considered lifting her and carrying her upstairs. He wondered how far he'd make it before having to put her down. Lifting her wouldn't be a problem, but the stairs might.

He was getting distracted by unimportant details. Mentally shaking himself, Ben deepened the kiss, his hands moving back to Anna's waist, sliding beneath her top until his skin touched hers.

She moaned into his mouth and pulled his shirt up, running her hands down his chest and lowering herself until they were eye level with one another.

'Do you want to go upstairs?' The words were out of his mouth before he could stop them, released the moment Anna broke the kiss to move her lips down to his chest.

She didn't even hesitate. Placing kisses down his body, she nodded and climbed off him somehow without her lips leaving the trail she was creating. As she reached the top of his jeans and Ben's breath caught in his throat, she stood and held out a hand.

'I think we should,' she told him. 'If you want to?'

Ben nodded and then glanced behind her.

'Can't really leave the fire,' he murmured, the sound of the sensible voice at the back of his head breaking through.

'Well, technically, we don't need to go upstairs,' came Anna's voice. Slowly, she kneeled on the carpet in front of him and gave him a questioning look.

Ben didn't think. He only nodded, his eyes widening as Anna went to undo his jeans.

He managed to stop a groan of frustration as her phone, on the table behind her, lit up and began ringing, buzzing against the tabletop.

Anna hesitated, considering Ben's still-clothed crotch, and then gave in and glanced at the phone behind her.

'Tell me that isn't your ex with another number?' Ben breathed, silently willing for Anna to silence the phone and put her attention back where it had been.

'I'm sorry,' she murmured, turning back to him holding the phone. The look in her eyes killed the mood, although it would take a little longer for Ben's body to get the message. He sagged back, exhaling hard.

'Why? What is it?'

'It's my mum. I have to take it.'

'Of course. Of course you do.'

Anna stood and gave Ben's groin a wistful look.

'I'll be quick.'

Ben nodded.

'Don't worry about it.'

She left the room and Ben glanced down at himself, suddenly exposed and silly on his sofa in front of the fire. Sitting up, he did up his jeans and straightened his clothing.

Sinking back against the sofa and staring into the fire, he couldn't help but listen to Anna on the phone to her mother, just behind him.

'Is everything all right?' came Anna's muffled voice.

Ben sighed, aware that he shouldn't be listening. He sipped at the remainder of his wine, still staring into the flames.

'What are you talking about? Of course I blocked him.'

Ben snapped his attention back to the conversation behind him.

'Why would you do that? What are you talking about? Mum!'

Anna's voice became quieter as she moved further away from Ben, deeper into the hallway.

'I can't believe you. This is my life! And I'm absolutely fine. Happy, in fact! Having a wonderful Christmas.'

Despite the polite voice in his head screaming at

him not to, Ben arched his back to lean closer to the door.

'Yes! A wonderful Christmas without you!' It sounded as if Anna wanted to scream, but it came out as a muted shout, a hushed anger that should have snapped Ben out of listening. Instead, he strained to hear more.

'You're meant to be on my side,' she was telling her mother. 'He cheated on me, Mum. He hurt me. You saw how much he hurt me. And I'm over him and I'm done. And now he's come slinking back into my life just because he's lost the things he left and hurt me for. And do you know why? Do you know why?' She shouted that last bit, and Ben jumped, trying to work out if she'd raised her voice or was approaching the living room. 'Because he knows I'm vulnerable right now.'

Ben sagged back into the sofa, staring down into his wine, his stomach churning. He placed the glass down.

'It doesn't matter, Mum. It's just...life stuff.' There came a pause and Anna gave the softest of sighs, but Ben heard it. He sat up, wondering if he should intervene. If they'd known each other longer than forty-eight hours, he might have done. If Anna was his and he was hers, he'd go and hold her at that moment, tell her she could hang up, that she was safe.

He stayed put, listening.

'No, Mum, I'm fine. Really. It's nothing.'

Another sigh and Ben's legs tingled with the need to march over to her and envelop her in warmth.

There was a long pause. Presumably, Anna's mother was talking.

'Okay. You won't talk to him again, right? Thank you. I appreciate that. Just block his number.' Another short sigh. 'Go into his details on your phone, scroll down and there's an option to block his number. Okay. Thank you.'

Another long pause, then soft footsteps as Anna approached the living room door.

'I'll talk to you tomorrow. Yes, I promise I'm good. I'm having fun. I'll speak to you tomorrow. Good night, Mum.'

In a panic, Ben grappled and grabbed at the remote on the table, pointing it at the TV just as Anna walked back into the room.

'I guess you heard that?'

'Only bits,' said Ben, realising the remote was the wrong way round and putting it back on the table. 'Are you all right?'

Anna shrugged, sitting beside him and reaching for her wine, which she downed in a single gulp.

'Not really. My mum's the one stirring things. Although she didn't start it, I don't think. Brad keeps sweet talking her, so she keeps blabbing information about me.'

'Like the fact that you're trapped in the snow, in a stranger's house?'

'With a man, yes.' Anna glanced at Ben. 'I'm sorry. For earlier. That was probably inappropriate.'

'Oh.'

'Wasn't it?'

'Well... Probably. If you're feeling vulnerable. I... I just want you to feel safe,' said Ben, avoiding her big eyes, not trusting that the wrong words wouldn't fall out.

'I guess,' said Anna quietly. 'I think I'm going to go to bed. Is that okay?'

'Of course. Whatever you need.'

They stayed on the sofa together, in silence, not looking at one another.

Then, slowly, Anna stood and began tidying up.

'Don't worry, I can do that,' said Ben.

Anna didn't argue. She nodded and walked out.

'Night,' she murmured as she went.

'Good night.'

Ben stared around the room, wondering what had just happened and whether he should be kicking himself for not handling that better. Shaking his head, he stood and tidied up. Washing up and wiping down the kitchen would help clear his thoughts. He couldn't go to bed until the fire had burned out, anyway.

15

Anna

While in the bathroom, brushing her teeth and preparing for bed, the rage in Anna grew. She wasn't vulnerable, why had she said she was? She was doing fine, thank you very much. And she'd been enjoying herself with Ben. She'd wanted to have sex with him.

Her body had gone from warm and tingly to crawling.

The rage burned a little brighter. Closing her bedroom door, Anna sat on the foot of the bed, still fully dressed, and became lost in thoughts of anger. This wasn't what this Christmas was supposed to be. She'd been so close to having a magical time, and once again, her family had ruined it. Her past had ruined it. She could have brought the magic back, returning to the living room and climbing back onto Ben's lap. But she hadn't.

Anna could scream.

She put her face in her hands and then smacked her knees. No. She wasn't going to be vulnerable or clumsy or stupid anymore. At least, not in that moment.

She was done.

Enough with Brad. She would block every number he came at her with.

She was done agreeing to everything her mother said, she would no longer be babysitting her half-siblings. Unless she chose to. It wasn't as if she didn't want a relationship with them. But it was time she stood up for herself.

Anna gave herself a defiant nod and then soften-ed, wondering what Ben was doing. Perhaps being interrupted had been the right thing. They barely knew each other.

The reality hit her in the chest like a snowball. Not even an hour earlier she'd been straddling a man she barely knew, kissing him, wanting his lips and hands on her, feeling his body respond to her.

Her stomach flipped, the warm, tingly sensation returning and spreading through her.

She hadn't needed the interruption, she doubted she would have regretted anything.

A soft knock on the bedroom door made her jump and snap her attention up.

'Anna?' came Ben's gentle voice.

Taking a deep breath, Anna stood and opened

the door, revealing Ben on the other side, hunched over a little, looking down at the floor.

'Erm, I just wanted to make sure you were okay? After all that. It didn't seem right. To just leave you. And... Yeah.' His gaze flicked up to hers and she held it.

She returned to the foot of her bed, sitting and patting the space beside her.

'I'm okay. Thanks. I'm really sorry about that.'

Ben entered the room and slowly sat beside her.

'Which bit?' he asked carefully.

The warmth in Anna grew, blooming in her chest as she looked up at Ben and smiled.

'When my mum called. Brad. All of that. Maybe I should just turn my phone off.'

Ben gave something of a smile.

'No, don't do that. You'll worry your mum even more. It's fine. The ex is a pain, sure, but I understand where your mum's coming from. Of course she's worried about you.'

Anna's smile fell and she looked down at her socked feet.

'But she's been talking to Brad. She's been letting him get to her. Can you believe she wants me to give him another chance?' Anna shook her head. 'I can't believe that. It's not like she doesn't know what he did.'

Frowning, Ben sat back a little.

'How did she react when you told her he'd cheated on you?'

Anna sighed, trying to remember.

'You know, I'm not sure she did. She was probably busy with the kids. Or work. Busy, busy, busy.' The warmth lessened and Anna sighed again, heavier this time, sitting back on the bed. 'I guess that's on me a little, then. I should have waited until she could pay me attention. It's just...'

'She's always busy?' Ben offered.

Anna nodded, glancing up at him.

'She doesn't get why I wanted this Christmas away from them all.' Tears stung at the back of her eyes. 'Oh, and when I say it like that, it's horrible, isn't it. I'm horrible. Wanting to spend Christmas away from my family.'

'You're not horrible.'

'No, no, I am. And I try to spend Christmas away from the people who love me and end up ruining your Christmas.' Anna sniffed, clenching her jaw, trying to stop her chin wobbling as the tears threatened to spill.

'You haven't ruined my Christmas,' came Ben's soft voice.

She looked up at him and, at the sight of her watery eyes, he raised an arm as if he was about to hug her. He thought better of it and placed the arm behind him so he could lean closer instead.

'Without you, my Christmas so far would have been me in that office working, in a dark, dingy house, eating whatever food I could be bothered to cook. Which wouldn't be much. With you here, the house looks beautiful. I'm out of my office. There's been great food. The house even smells better because of all that.'

'I spilled wine on your carpet,' Anna said quietly.

'And then you somehow got the stain out.'

'I turned off the electricity.'

'Because of my uncle's old fairy lights.'

'I set off your smoke alarms.'

'Because of my old oven. This whole house needs doing up. None of those things were your fault.'

'Except the wine.'

There it was. That rare smile taking over from Ben's frown, his face slowly lighting up. Anna smiled back, brushing away the tears in her eyes.

'Without you, there wouldn't have been kissing,' said Ben gently.

'And the kissing was good?' she said quietly.

Ben nodded.

'I thought so. Did you?'

Anna agreed.

'And then I spoiled it all by answering my phone.'

'Because your mum called. If my mum had called, I'd have answered the phone too. It's family.'

Something caught at Anna's mind and she gave him a thoughtful look.

'Has your mum called? It's Christmas Eve.'

Ben shook his head.

'I'll speak to her tomorrow, I'm sure. You haven't spoken to your dad.'

'He's on holiday.' Anna waved the notion away. 'I'll speak to him tomorrow. That was always the plan.'

'Right. And I'm not the one stranded in a stranger's house because of the snow. My mum doesn't have a reason to call me yet.' Ben's smile faded and Anna's chest tightened as his frown returned. 'Maybe the kissing was a mistake. You're in a stranger's house, cut off by the snow.'

'No. No.' Anna shook her head and moved closer to Ben, bending to catch his eye. 'You're not a stranger. I mean, yes, we haven't known each other for long. What I mean is, you don't feel like a stranger. Not anymore. Maybe... Maybe you never did. Well, okay, you did. Right at the beginning, but not anymore.'

'It's been two days,' Ben pointed out, but the corners of his lips were twitching up. 'I know what you mean, though. When you were talking with your mum, I just wanted to...'

'You wanted to what?' Anna prodded when Ben hesitated for too long.

'Hug you. Hold you.' Ben shrugged. 'I didn't want you going through that. The anger and feeling...vulnerable.'

'I don't feel vulnerable,' Anna told him. 'I don't know why I said that. You wanted to hold me?'

Ben nodded, glancing up at her.

'That sounds nice.' Anna searched his eyes, her mouth dry.

Slowly, a little awkwardly, Ben shuffled closer and wrapped his arms around her. She held him close, breathing in his warmth and a hint of his cologne.

'You're so warm,' she said into his chest, listening to him breath.

'That's being in the room with the fire,' he murmured, his voice rumbling through her.

'Is the fire out?'

'Yeah.'

'Good.' Anna's eyes drifted shut and she opened them quickly. This was no position to fall asleep in. Apart from anything else, her back was at a strange angle and was already starting to ache. Perhaps feeling the same, Ben shuffled his position.

Anna pulled out of the hug and checked his jumper for eye makeup stains. He was clean. Clean and warm and safe.

Anna smiled at him and lay back on the bed. After a moment's consideration, he lay beside her and they stared up at the ceiling.

'This house would look amazing with a freshen up,' she murmured. 'I love that ceiling rose, but it could do with painting.'

'So could the whole house,' said Ben, tilting his head and sighing. 'If I had the money. Or the time. Or both.' He turned to look at her. 'Or had someone in my life who was good at those things.'

She turned to look him in the eye.

'Because spilling red wine on your carpet makes

you think I'll be good at painting?'

Anna's heart skipped as Ben smiled. It was a strange, lopsided smile thanks to their positioning.

'You made the living room beautiful.'

'Anyone with fairy lights can make a room beautiful,' said Anna, knowing immediately that wasn't true.

Ben shook his head.

'I think you could make this house beautiful,' he murmured, glancing down at her lips. 'You have the vision for it.'

'You want me in your life to make your house beautiful?' she asked gently, moving closer.

'I think I just want you in my life generally,' he breathed.

Anna pushed forward until their lips met.

Unlike on the sofa, this kiss was gentle and slow. They breathed each other in and, after a minute, Ben wrapped his arm around Anna's waist.

'Hmm.' Anna broke the kiss. 'Just to make your house beautiful, or more than that?'

Ben grinned and shook his head. The sight of such a wide smile on his face made Anna's chest flutter.

'More,' he murmured.

'You should smile more,' she told him. 'You have an incredible smile.'

Ben leaned close and caught her lips in his.

She wasn't sure how long they lay there kissing, hands gently lifting clothes to explore beneath.

Tepid fingers against hot skin.

It didn't go further, despite Anna wanting it to. She wanted to climb on top of Ben, to strip off her clothes and then his, but every time she tried to muster the energy her body would refuse and her eyes would become heavy.

The kissing stopped and they found themselves looking into one another's eyes, Ben gently stroking Anna's long hair.

'Are you cold?' he asked, his voice somehow both sleepy and husky.

'A little,' she said, stifling a yawn. 'Only when I move away from you.'

'Stay there.' He pressed a kiss against her forehead and left the bed, leaving behind a large, cold chasm beside her. She missed him immediately. Then it went dark as the light was turned out and a thick blanket was thrown over her. Ben was back, sliding in beside her.

'You know, we could just get into bed properly,' Anna said as Ben lay on his back and beckoned for Anna to cuddle up. She did so, resting her head on his chest, snuggling into his warm jumper. She could just make out the beating of his heart, his chest rising and dropping as he breathed.

'I like this,' said Ben, kissing her hair and wrapping his arms around her.

If anything, she was now too warm, but she didn't complain. Sleep came over her quickly. She slid a hand beneath Ben's clothes, to rest on his warm chest, skin to skin. His thumb stroked her back, at the hem of her top, sometimes brushing beneath.

Anna smiled into him.

'I like this too,' she mustered, before sleep over-whelmed her.

16

Ben

Ben woke the next morning shivering. Eyes open, he tried to judge the time, but the room seemed as dark as it had been when he'd brought the blanket over to Anna, lying on the bed. She was asleep beside him, the blanket wrapped around her.

Smiling, Ben watched her, replaying the previous night in his mind.

While he regretted her mother's phone call interrupting them, he thought he preferred the night they'd had. Cuddling, falling asleep wrapped around one another.

Taking care not to wake Anna, Ben slipped off the bed and checked the time. It was quarter past six; his internal clock didn't care that it was Christmas Day.

Sure that Anna wouldn't want to be woken so

early, Ben found another blanket. He removed his jumper and t-shirt and climbed back beside Anna, throwing the blanket over them both. Snaking an arm around her waist, she moved back into him in her sleep until they were spooning. Ben breathed in her hair and closed his eyes, wanting to remember this moment.

He must have fallen asleep because Ben woke to find Anna watching him.

'Morning,' she murmured, sinking down beneath the blankets.

'Merry Christmas.' Ben stretched and yawned, blinking as he looked around the room. It had been a while since he'd woken to a light room. His gaze landed back on Anna and she gave an awkward smile.

'Merry Christmas.' She rolled off the bed and stretched her arms above her head. 'Not a re-commended way to sleep,' she said, opening the curtains a little.

'Is it still snowing?'

Anna sighed.

'Not as heavy as it was.' She turned back to Ben, hugging herself. 'I'm just going to, erm, use the bathroom.'

'Okay.'

Ben watched her leave and deflated into the bed. What had that been about? He'd been hoping for a morning snuggle beneath the blankets. If he'd known Anna would feel so awkward waking beside him, he'd have gotten up when he woke before six and… Probably gone and done some work in his office.

He sighed and rubbed his eyes, hoping to smash some sense into himself. It was a ridiculous way to live, always working, even on Christmas Day. He needed more people around him, and if Anna didn't want to be one of those people then the new year offered a chance to meet someone else. Maybe he'd give those dating apps a try. He'd never had the courage before.

Anna jogged back into the room and hopped onto the bed, grabbing the blankets and curling up beside Ben, shivering against him.

Slowly, he wrapped an arm around her, finding her clothing cold to the touch.

'You all right?'

'Yes. I'm freezing.' Anna lifted and brushed her lips against his, leaving the distinct minty taste of toothpaste.

Frowning, Ben looked down at her.

'Did you just go brush your teeth?'

Anna pressed her lips together.

'Well, yeah. Because, you know. Morning breath.' She snuggled back up against his bare chest. 'Why?'

'I thought you regretted last night,' said Ben, staring up at the ceiling, not even fighting against a smile.

'What? Of course I didn't! We need to stop this.'

Anna lifted until she was propping herself over Ben. 'If I don't want to do something, I'll tell you. If I don't like something or regret something, I'll tell you. Okay?'

'Okay. It's just—'

'I know, I know. I obviously didn't do that with my ex but I've learned from that, and I want things to be different with you.'

Anna's smile grew as Ben grinned. Watching her face light up was like nothing else.

'You want things to be different with me?' he murmured.

'Yeah. Do you?'

Ben didn't even think about it. He nodded, pulling her down for a hard kiss before remembering that he hadn't brushed his teeth.

'Hang on.' Gently pushing her away, Ben escaped to the en suite in his bedroom, where his toothbrush was. Anna was right, the house was freezing. He'd soon fix that. He'd start a fire, maybe while Anna prepared a breakfast. They could cook Christmas dinner together and watch Christmas films and TV specials, cuddled together on the sofa. Maybe they'd just leave the TV on and become distracted with one another. Make their way to the bedroom, get under the covers, warm each other up.

Ben rushed back to Anna and climbed beneath the blankets, kissing her as if he'd been gone for hours.

Anna laughed, pulling him closer until she was on her back and he was over her. His hand slid down her body and back up, finding the hem of her top.

'Your hands are like ice,' she told him, kissing his lower lip as she instinctively flinched away from his touch.

'Sorry.' Ben kept his hands over her clothes as he kissed down to her neck. Anna made a noise that set his body alight. His hand found her breast and she made another noise, even better than the last. Moaning into her neck, Ben breathed her in, not wanting anything to ruin this moment.

'What's that noise?' Anna whispered in his ear.

'You. And I think it's my new favourite noise,' he said, his voice muffled by the hot skin of her neck.

'No.' Anna giggled, pushing him away a little. '*That* noise.'

Forced away from her, Ben stopped and listened, trying to hear past the sound of his own pounding heart.

'Oh, that's my phone ringing. Ignore it.' He lowered himself back to her neck, kissing down to her collarbone.

'What if it's urgent?'

'It's someone in my family calling to wish me a happy Christmas. Ignore it.'

'Are you sure?'

Ben was about to dip his mouth down to Anna's clothed breast when his brain decided to flash images of his family in peril before him.

Groaning, he slipped off the bed, reluctantly leaving Anna behind.

'Fine. Hang on. Don't move. Hold whatever thought you have.'

Anna laughed and shooed him away. He paused for a moment, staring at her, trying to remember where he'd left his phone. As he thought, Anna smiled and slowly, purposefully, pulled her top over her head and unclasped her bra, revealing her bare chest.

All thoughts vanished from Ben's head.

'I thought you wanted me to get the phone,' he breathed, staring at her.

'Just something to make you hurry back.'

'I'll call them back later,' Ben told her, approaching the bed.

'No! No. Go see who it is. Just in case.' Anna covered her chest. 'These will be waiting for you when you come back.'

Ben grinned and kissed Anna gently on the lips before rushing from the room.

This was shaping up to be the best Christmas he'd ever had, and it turned out he didn't need the wrapping paper or roast potatoes or even the tree and twinkling lights.

His phone was in his bedroom, waiting for him on the bedside table and flashing a name. That was strange, it should have gone to voicemail by now.

All thoughts of Anna and her breasts left him

and he checked the name before answering.

'Mum? Is everything okay?'

'Merry Christmas!'

Ben stopped and waited for more.

'Merry Christmas,' he said carefully. 'Are you all right? I've got two missed calls from you.'

'Of course. I just wondered where you were? I was worried something had happened.'

If only Ben had a chance for something to happen.

'I'm home. I'm fine. I just left my phone upstairs, that's all. Can I give you a call back later? It's just I'm kind of in the middle of something and—'

'Not yet, hang on. Are you sitting down?'

Ben sat on his bed.

'Why? What's going on?'

'I don't want you to panic.'

'Then tell me what's going on so I won't panic.' All sorts of ideas were flashing through Ben's mind. Who could be ill in the family? Had a young cousin been out drinking and driving? Had there been an accident, or incident?

'I just found out that your brother is in hospital.'

Ben's chest ached. He put a hand to it, as if that would help.

'Why? What's wrong?'

'It's nothing bad. He had stomach pains all yesterday and started vomiting. He was rushed into surgery to have his appendix out. I'm just waiting to hear back from Mali. She's going to wait until he's woken up, but so far we know everything went well.'

'Jeez, Mum. And that's how you chose to tell me?' Ben almost screeched.

'Well, how else should I tell you?'

'Stewart has appendicitis and had surgery last night.'

'I don't think it was last night. Just yesterday. Because of the time difference, and—'

'Whatever! You made me think something really awful had happened.'

'Well, it might do. He's in good hands, I think, but still. Stuff happens after surgery, you know.'

'Mum!'

'I'm sorry. I should have worded it better. Anyway, how is your Christmas so far? What are you in the middle of? Are you peeling sprouts? Is that what I've interrupted with news of your brother?'

Ben blinked and thought furiously for an appropriate response.

'Yes, Mum. I was peeling sprouts.'

'Good. Then you have time for a chat?'

Ben rubbed a hand down his face and stood, walking slowly back to Anna's room where she was waiting on the foot of the bed. She was holding up a blanket to cover herself and gave him a concerned look when he appeared in the doorway.

'A quick chat,' Ben relented, realising the moment had passed. 'Sure.'

Anna gave a small, sweet smile and stood, dropping the blanket. Ben's pulse quickened and Anna wandered over, lifting up on tiptoe to kiss his cheek.

'I'm going to have a shower. See you downstairs?' she whispered.

Ben nodded, tearing his gaze from her bare breasts to her eyes. She winked at him and then vanished into the bathroom.

His mother was going on about what she'd gotten up to on Christmas Eve and she snapped Ben back to the room, asking, 'I saw on the news that you have snow? Some freak storm or something. How is it there?'

His gut twisting at the lost opportunity, Ben gathered himself and returned to his room to give Anna some privacy.

'Yeah, currently snowed in. And it's still falling.' He checked out the window as he spoke, watching the light flakes against the glass. 'But it's not as heavy.'

'And you're all right? Got everything you need? Are you warm?'

'Everything's fine, Mum. I've got everything I need.' He sat on his bed with a smile; he'd never meant that more in his life. A shiver made him retrieve a clean t-shirt and the Christmas jumper his sister had given him.

By the time Ben ended the call with his mother, Anna was out of the shower but still in the bathroom. He considered knocking, to see if he could be invited in. For a few minutes, his mind was preoccupied by the idea of her hot, damp skin. Shaking his head, Ben stripped off his clothes and walked into his en suite to have a shower of his own. If it wasn't for the snow outside and the creeping chill in the house, he would have made it a cold one.

Fully dressed, he walked downstairs, following the smell of frying bacon, and stopped at the sight of wrapped presents under the tree in the living room.

'How...?' He looked at Anna in the kitchen. Her long hair was washed and still wet, and she wore an ugly Christmas jumper, holding a spatula in one hand.

'What do you mean, how? Santa's been!' She grinned. 'Bacon roll for breakfast?'

Ben stared at her.

'How did you do all this?' He stepped into the kitchen as she brandished her spatula at him.

'Christmas magic! Do you want a coffee?'

'Sure. I'll make it. Do you want one?'

'Please. Take them into the living room, I'll follow you. Red or brown sauce?'

'Brown for me.'

Ben made the coffees, bewildered. He was staring at the presents when Anna joined him, sitting beside him on the sofa and handing him a bacon roll on a plate.

'Christmas breakfast of dreams,' she said, taking a bite.

'Where did the presents come from?'

'Well,' said Anna around her mouthful. 'We need something to open on Christmas and it's not like we knew we'd be spending today together. So I improvised and put some presents together.'

Ben frowned, studying the different shapes.

'What are they?'

'That's the point of unwrapping.' Anna elbowed him playfully. 'But we have to be quick. Most of them are parts of Christmas dinner and I don't want them to spoil.'

Laughing, Ben took a bite of his roll and then reached for the first present, handing it to Anna.

They unwrapped them together, which was easy enough. Anna hadn't had much time while Ben was in the shower, so they weren't wrapped well. As they unwrapped each one, they would dart back to the kitchen to place things in the fridge or on the counter, ready for cooking later.

'Last one,' said Anna, handing Ben a piece of paper folded over.

'What's this? The receipt?'

'No. An actual present. From me to you.'

Ben looked up into Anna's eyes, lit up by her beautiful smile.

Heart beating hard against his ribs, he unfolded the piece of paper and read the note she'd given him.

This is permission to do no work today or tomorrow.

Ben read it three times, lingering on the kisses.

'Thank you,' he murmured, reaching over to kiss her lips. She gave him two quick kisses and then reached for a red bow, saved from the wrapped Christmas dinner ingredients. Placing it on her head, she held out her arms to him.

'Are you my other present?' he asked, grinning.

Anna nodded and the bow fell off. Ben quickly snatched it up and placed it on his own head.

'This is permission to carry on where we left off earlier,' he told her. 'And thank you. For all of this. You're amazing.'

Anna leaned forward and kissed him slowly, the bow sliding and falling from his head.

'I'm going to start cooking. Do you want to start the fire and then join me, make sure I don't burn the house down?'

Ben wasn't quite over that kiss. Their noses were close enough to touch, so he only nodded.

'I mean it,' he whispered. 'You're amazing.'

'You haven't tasted my roast yet,' said Anna, kissing him and then standing and leaving the room.

Ben considered that statement and, smiling to himself, heaved himself to his feet to sort the fire out.

17

Anna

This wasn't quite how Anna had imagined cooking Christmas dinner that year; it was even better. Every year, when visiting family, she would offer to help in the kitchen and would be told to watch the children. This year she had dreamed of cooking in the little cottage kitchen, making everything just to her taste. Now, she was working in a bigger kitchen, asking the gorgeous man who owned it how he liked his potatoes, what his favourite part of Christmas dinner was, what time they should be eating.

Every time Ben passed her, he would put a hand on her waist, his fingers lingering. Every time she passed him, she would kiss his shoulder, through his jumper, and relish the sparks that flew through her body.

'Your poor brother. When do you think you'll find out more?' Anna asked as she peeled the carrots.

'I emailed his wife, Mali. I'll give her a call in a bit, see what's going on.' Ben put the turkey in the oven. 'Right. That's done. What else can I do?'

'No, no, you go call your family.'

'Okay.'

Ben hesitated and then kissed Anna's cheek before leaving the kitchen. There was nothing she could do to keep the smile from her face.

As she peeled another carrot, she gazed out of the window at the snow. The sky was still a blanket of light-grey cloud but the snow was easing, falling in fluttering flakes instead of icy sheets. The garden was thick with it, the outlines of trees and shrubs blurred. She tried to imagine how it might look in the summer, green and full of flowers, perhaps. Trees lined the back of the garden and she wondered whether beyond there were fields or another person's garden. The snow made the house seem so sheltered, as if there were no neighbours.

She was still smiling as she turned her attention from the carrots to the potatoes.

The kitchen was warming up, but there was still something missing. Anna paused to dig out her phone and put on a Christmas playlist. The music filled the room and Anna turned it down so it was in the background. Still, there was something missing.

'A dog,' she murmured to herself, glancing at the

peeled and chopped carrots. 'Lying in their bed at the back of the kitchen.' She glanced behind her, finding just the right spot. 'Coming out to sit beside me and wait for a bit of carrot.'

That was it. Snow in the garden, Christmas music gently playing as she prepared Christmas dinner while Ben spoke to his family across the world. Dog at her feet. Maybe a child, too. A baby in a highchair. A young child playing with the toys they'd unwrapped at four o'clock that morning. Even a sullen teenager, sitting at the table, as Anna told them yet again how she'd met their father, as she did every Christmas.

Anna sighed wistfully, staring out at the snow-laden garden.

'Ouch!'

She jumped away and cried out before she fully registered the pain.

'Oh, for the love of—' Anna reached for a piece of kitchen towel to wrap around where the knife had sliced into her finger instead of the potato. She dabbed at the blood and checked the wound, praying to whoever was listening that it wasn't too deep.

No. It didn't need stitches, but it was nasty and the sight of it made it hurt more.

She kept the kitchen towel wrapped around it, applying pressure and held her hand above her head. Once she was happy that the bleeding had stopped, she washed the wound and considered what to do next. She had a little first aid kit, but it was in her car and she didn't fancy wrapping up and going out into the snow just for one little plaster.

'Ah!' She rushed into the hallway where her coat was hanging and dug her good hand into a pocket. Out came a packet of tissues, a dog poo bag even though she didn't have a dog, a pack of mints and two plasters.

She'd slid them into her pocket on a breezy day in the autumn, when she'd gone for a walk through the woods with her father and his family. It had been raining and the ground was slippery with mud and leaves, and Anna knew from past experiences that it was inevitable that she'd fall over. Even with the hiking boots she'd bought for herself as a birthday present for such occasions.

She washed her hands and placed the plaster over the small wound, making sure it wasn't too tight. Then she cleaned the knife and went back to peeling and chopping potatoes, crisis averted.

The smile was soon back on her face, imagining how the dog would have followed her into the hallway and back, how the baby would have grumbled, how the teenager would have rolled their eyes.

How Ben would share that eye roll and kiss her finger better when he returned to the kitchen and spotted the plaster.

Anna stopped and glanced back into the hallway, wondering if Ben would appear at that moment. He didn't.

It was only then that Anna considered how

strange these thoughts were. How comfortable she felt, not just in the strange house but with this man she hardly knew. As if she'd known him for years. She looked back up to the garden. Did that mean something?

Her smile broke into a grin.

It had to mean something.

The grin faded as she returned her attention to the vegetables and spotted the plaster on her finger. She couldn't get too complacent; that was when the universe would throw something at her. Something would go wrong. It always did.

When she'd first met Brad, she'd thought the world of him. But had she ever imagined a baby and a dog in their future this vividly?

Anna caught herself staring at her own fingers.

She'd barely daydreamed about starting a family with Brad, although they'd talked about it. It had been a consideration, never really a daydream. She didn't want any of that with Brad. He wouldn't have rolled his eyes lovingly and kissed her hurt finger, he'd have verbally chastised her and asked for a beer.

Then again, Ben hadn't actually walked in and rolled his eyes before kissing her finger, either. Not yet.

A small beep paused the music momentarily and Anna welcomed the distraction, checking her phone. A merry Christmas message from her dad. Smiling again, Anna picked up her phone and messaged him back. She'd call him later, she was sure, and then she remembered that he didn't know that she wasn't in her cosy Christmas cottage.

Pressing her lips together, she added 'Are you free?' to the end of her message and hit send.

Her phone rang almost immediately and Anna took a deep breath before answering.

'Hi, Dad.'

'Merry Christmas, Annie! How's the cottage?'

'Merry Christmas! Erm, well, I didn't actually make it to the cottage.'

'Oh, so you're at your mum's? It's very quiet there. Are you hiding somewhere?'

Anna could hear her father's smile. She wondered if it would drop when she told him what had happened. Did she have to tell him?

'No. I'm not at Mum's. Erm... I'm actually... With a friend.' Anna glanced back to the kitchen door and the empty hallway.

'Oh? Is everything all right?'

'Yes, yes, everything's fine. Great, even.'

'What made you change your mind? Just the idea of Christmas alone?'

'Not exactly. Have you heard about the freak snow we've had?'

'No!'

'Well, we had a freak snowstorm. And it's been going on for days. It started when I was driving up to the cottage.'

'Oh no. Please tell me nothing happened.'

'Well, the car broke down just before I reached the village.'

'Oh, Annie.'

'And the SatNav took me down this little country road. In the heavy snow.'

'And you listened to it?'

'It's the only road into the village.' Anna sighed.

'Of course,' her father muttered. 'Oh, Anna, I'm so sorry. Where are you, then? Tell me you're safe.'

'I'm perfectly safe, very warm, currently making Christmas dinner. Everything's fine.'

'Where are you then?'

Anna bit her lip.

'Well, as I said I was on a country road. My phone reception went.'

'Of course it did.'

'So I knocked on a door to see if they had a land-line.'

'And?'

'And he did. So I called breakdown.'

There was a pause and then her father slowly said, 'But?'

'But they couldn't come out. Because of the snow and because I was safe. So I called the man with the keys to the cottage.'

Her father sighed down the phone. 'And?'

'And he couldn't come out either, but he knows the man who lives here and said he's very nice. Well, he knew his uncle. But niceness runs in the family, so it's fine.'

There was a long pause. Anna's mouth went dry and she checked the empty hallway again. 'Dad?'

'So, you're in the middle of nowhere in the house of a strange man?'

He was definitely not smiling anymore.

'Technically, yes. But Ben is lovely.'

'Oh, Ben, is it?'

'Yes. He's been such a gentleman. Very respectful, very kind, and—'

'And you're staying in his house?'

'Yes. The house is huge. It's called the Old Vicarage. He gave me a spare room at the complete opposite end of the house to his room. And my own bathroom.'

'How old is this Ben?'

'I... I don't know. My age? A bit older, maybe. Why?'

'Anna, what if he's a murderer? Or worse?'

'I know, Dad, but he's not. I promise. He's lovely and kind, and you'll like him!'

'Like him? When am I going to meet him?'

Anna snapped her mouth shut.

'I don't know,' she murmured carefully. 'I just mean, you would like him, if you ever met him.' She clenched her eyes shut, silently reprimanding herself. 'Anyway, I'm absolutely fine.'

'Does your mum know about this?'

'Yes.'

'And is she okay with it?'

'Erm... She's threatened to come get me a few

times. But she can't, because of the snow.'

'Is it still snowing?' her father asked.

Anna looked out of the window.

'A little. Very gently. Nowhere near as heavy. I'll probably be able to leave soon,' she said, a heavy ball dropping into her stomach.

'Good. If you need help, then call the police. Or send me a message. I'll call the police. Send me the details of where you are.'

'Dad, I promise, I'm fine.'

'Still, send me the address of this house.'

'Fine. And I'll let you know that I'm still alive at regular intervals, shall I?'

'Yes, please!'

There was another pause and Anna started smiling, listening to her father considering all that information.

'You like this strange man, huh?' he asked quietly.

'I do.'

'Snowed in with a strange man at Christmas.' He tutted. 'Sounds like one of those books your mum likes.'

Anna laughed.

'Do me a favour and tell her that next time you talk to her and she goes on about all this. She's already been talking to Brad.'

'Brad? Who's Brad? Oh, wait. Brad? Your ex, Brad? That muppet? Why is she talking to him? I hope she's giving him a piece of her mind.'

'Not exactly.'

Her father sighed down the phone again.

'Brad's been trying to call me, but I blocked him,' she added.

'Good!'

Anna smiled to herself.

'Ben told me to block him. After I explained who Brad is and what he'd done.'

There came another long pause.

'That doesn't mean he isn't a murderer, Annie.'

'I know, Dad.'

'Where is this Ben now?'

'Calling his sister-in-law, I think. He's talking to his family. His brother's in hospital in Thailand.'

'On holiday?'

'No, he lives there. Appendicitis.'

'Nasty. Poor guy. Okay, well, your Christmas is going well so far with this strange, kind man?'

'It is. I'm actually having a better one than I thought I'd have in the cosy cottage on my own.'

'That's good.'

'How about you, Dad? How's it going there?'

'Magical. It's freezing cold, everything's white with snow and we saw the Northern Lights yester-day.'

'Dad! I'm so jealous. I bet we have as much snow, though.'

'Doubt it!'

'I'll send you a photo.'

'Sure, and I'll send you a photo of the Northern

Lights.'

They chatted a little longer, until Anna made her excuses and said goodbye. She stared at her blank phone screen once they'd hung up. Her father had never taken her anywhere as exciting as Iceland to see the Northern Lights. Family holidays had been caravans in Cornwall, but these days he took his wife and children to exclusive hotels in the sun and dog sledding in Iceland to stay in glass rooms beneath the Arctic sky.

Anna bit her lip and reminded herself that her father hadn't had the career he had now. They hadn't had the money to afford such holidays. Caravans in Cornwall had given her wonderful memories of playing catch with her father on the beach, eating ice cream looking out to sea, watching the rain fall at the pub window while they played card games.

She wondered briefly if her half-siblings were making those kinds of memories?

The Northern Lights were probably wasted on the young. Anna nodded in an attempt to convince herself. She'd much prefer to see them in a romantic setting. She checked the empty hallway for Ben one last time and then returned to preparing the food.

18

Ben

'Mum? I just spoke to Mali,' said Ben, slowly twirling his office chair round with his feet. 'Stu's out of surgery and doing well.'

'I told you that,' said his mother.

'Right. Well, it's been longer and he's still doing well.' Ben sighed. 'I wish they were closer,' he added quietly.

'It is what it is. It would be nice if we were all closer. Merry Christmas, sweetheart.'

'Merry Christmas, Mum. How's it going there?'

'All right. We had a light lunch and a nice walk by the sea. The sun is shining and it's lovely and warm. How's the snow?'

'Still white, crisp and even.'

'But you're safe? You have heat and food?'

'Yes, Mum. I'm fine. Got all the Christmas food,

heating's working fine. Everything's working, actually. We're lucky, I guess.'

'We?'

'I'm lucky.' Ben squeezed his eyes shut for a moment.

'So, you're snowed in?'

'Yup.'

'Snowed in for Christmas. How romantic. If only you had someone to share it with.' His mother sighed down the phone. 'Sorry. I didn't mean that.'

'It's okay.' Ben chewed his bottom lip, considering his options. 'Actually, I am sharing this Christmas with someone.' He snapped his mouth shut.

'What? Who? Do you have a girlfriend you haven't told me about?'

'No. No, it's not like that,' said Ben, his pulse quickening at the thought of Anna being labelled his girlfriend. 'Her car broke down in the snow and mine was the closest house.'

There was a pause, which grew longer, the silence stretching out, until Ben wondered if he'd made a mistake mentioning any of this to his mother. 'Mum?'

'So, you're saying,' said his mother, slowly, 'that there's a strange woman in your house right now because she broke down outside in the snow?'

'Yes.'

'And you let her in? Why? Because it's Christmas?'

'I let her in to use the landline. She didn't have

any reception to call the breakdown service.'

'Okay.'

'But they couldn't come out. Because of the snowstorm.'

'Right.'

'She's meant to be staying in a cottage on the other side of the village.'

'So why didn't she get whoever she was staying with to come get her?'

'Because she was going on her own.'

'So, there's a strange woman who was planning a Christmas alone in a cottage in your house, right now?'

'Yes.' Ben frowned. What his mother was saying was true, but the tone made it sound ridiculous. 'She can't get to the cottage, Mum. Because of the snow.'

'And I suppose she can't go home, because of the snow?'

'She lives down south.'

'Of course she does.'

Ben sighed, gritting his teeth a little.

'She's really lovely, Mum.'

'Oh, I'm sure she is. She's found a single man with a big house to mooch off over Christmas.'

'It's not like that.' Ben rubbed his face. 'She needed help. And it's Christmas!'

'What if she's scamming you, Ben?'

'She's not. I promise. I've seen her car, we've talked a lot. She's not tricking me or anything, she's just a really nice person.'

'If you say so. I just want you to be safe.'

'You didn't think I had all those thoughts? Of course I did. But she's genuine, Mum. I promise. Everything is fine.'

There was another pause, although Ben hardly noticed. He stared at his blank computer screen, wishing he was back in the kitchen with Anna.

'Okay. I just... I worry about you.'

'I know, Mum. But you don't need to.'

'After everything's that happened, I don't want you to get hurt again.'

'She's only staying until it stops snowing and breakdown come and fix her car, or until the man with the cottage keys can come give her a lift. Whichever happens first, I guess.'

'That's not what I meant.'

Ben jolted out of his thoughts.

'What did you mean?'

'I mean, I worry about you getting into a new relationship and getting hurt.'

'I—'

'Don't. Don't even start denying it. I can hear it in your voice. Ben Wilmslow does not just let people into that house of his. Your little fortress of solitude, isn't that what your sister calls it? So this woman must be something. Maybe she's pretty or whatever, but there must be something about her. And while I'm happy for you to pursue all of that because I want you to be happy, I also don't want you to get hurt. All right?'

A smile tugged at the corners of Ben's mouth.

'All right. Thank you, Mum.'

'So, you do like her?'

Ben shrugged, even though his mother couldn't see it.

'There's something about her.'

His mother laughed, loud enough that he had the pull the phone from his ear a little.

'Good. Well, take care of her, but most of all, take care of yourself. Don't let her take advantage. Yes?'

'I won't, Mum.'

'What's this woman doing now, anyway?'

'Cooking Christmas dinner.'

'You should go help her, then.'

'Yeah. I should.'

Ben flinched as there came the sound of a baking tray crashing into something from the other side of the house. 'I really should. Merry Christmas, Mum. Enjoy the sunshine.'

'Be careful in the snow, sweetheart.'

Ben hung up and sent a quick message to his father, wishing him a merry Christmas and telling him to call when he was free. Then he strode through the house, back to the kitchen.

'Everything all right?'

'Fine!' said Anna, smiling and glancing over her shoulder to Ben. 'I dropped a baking tray, but no harm done.' She held up her hands as if to prove it and Ben spotted the plaster on her finger.

'That's new. What happened?' He approached without thinking.

'Oh, I'm fine. Sliced my finger open when chopping up a potato.'

'Is it deep?' Ben held out his hand for her, although there was nothing to see. Just a plaster wrapped around her finger.

'No, it's fine. I cleaned it and I carry plasters with me. Because, you know, I'm me.'

Without thinking, Ben lifted her hand to his lips and kissed the tip of her injured finger. A subtle but visible shiver ran through Anna, and she stepped closer to him, looking up into his eyes.

'Mum thinks you're going to either scam me out of my money and home or break my heart,' he told her gently.

'My dad thinks you might be a murderer, or worse.'

Ben flinched.

'Oh, don't worry. I told him you were neither of those things. And that you're an amazing kisser.'

Anna laughed at Ben's horrified, widening eyes.

'You didn't?'

'Of course I didn't!' she assured him. 'And I'm not here to scam you or hurt you.'

'I know. I told my mum that,' Ben said quietly, watching her. 'Can I help with anything?' he asked, not taking his eyes from her.

Anna smiled, a small smile that made Ben's stomach flip.

'Nope. Everything's under control.' She went up on tiptoe and pressed her lips against his.

'Did you really tell your dad we kissed?'

'No! Did you tell your mum?'

'No. Although, she sort of guessed, I think.'

Anna gave Ben the same horrified look he'd just given her.

'She guessed that we kissed?'

Ben shook his head.

'Only that I want to kiss you.'

Glancing over at him, Anna gave Ben the kind of smile that made him want to press his lips hard against hers, wrap his arms around her and lift her onto the worktop. He swallowed.

'Do you want to kiss me now?' she asked.

Ben only nodded.

'Do you think this is strange?' Anna whispered as Ben looked down at her, thinking furiously.

'What?'

'This? Us? I turn up at your door, broken down car and heavy snow, and you're so kind to me. And then, this just feels so...'

'Easy,' Ben breathed.

Anna nodded, her smile growing.

'Do you feel that too?'

'I do. When you first turned up, I just wanted you out of my house. But now...' He glanced down to her lips. 'I like you being here. I've never found it this easy to talk to someone, which is ridiculous. We don't know each other, do we.'

'It's probably the snow. And the twinkly lights,' said Anna.

'I think I wanted to kiss you before you put the lights up,' Ben admitted.

'Before I blew the electricity, you mean? And that didn't put you off?' Anna grinned, and Ben found himself laughing.

'Do you know how long it's been since I've felt this way?' he murmured, snaking an arm around her waist. 'Even if it doesn't last. Even if we find out we actually don't like each other. Thank you for this.'

Warmth shot through him as Anna placed a hand on his chest.

'What if it does last?' she asked so quietly Ben almost couldn't make out the words.

He couldn't think about that. Not properly.

'A Christmas miracle,' he told her, leaning down and brushing his lips over hers.

'Us being together would be a miracle?' she asked, moving away enough to speak before he could continue kissing her.

'Your car breaking down right outside my house as the snow was falling. We never get snow in December,' he breathed, moving towards her and catching her lips in his again.

This time she didn't pull away. She wrapped her arms around his neck and pulled him closer.

'You're going to break my heart, aren't you,' she murmured.

'I will do everything in my power not to,' he told her, shocking himself as he realised just how much he meant that. The shock meant he hesitated, and Anna looked up at him.

'Already regretting saying that?' she half-laughed.

'No. Amazed at how much I mean it,' he told her, studying her features, looking deep into her eyes and wondering if she was really the person he felt he knew her to be.

Anna softened.

'Sorry,' he added. 'Sorry, that was too much.'

Anna shook her head.

'The amazing thing is that it really isn't too much,' she told him, pulling him back down to kiss him.

The oven making a noise broke them apart, and Ben moved to check it wasn't about to set itself on fire. When he turned back, Anna was watching him, running her fingers through her now dry hair. She glanced behind him and her eyes widened.

'What?'

Ben turned to look at what she'd seen, his mind offering images of strangers at the window. Instead, his empty garden stared back at him. He frowned. 'What is it?'

'It's stopped snowing,' came Anna's gentle voice.

Another heavy ball fell into the pit of Ben's stomach.

'Oh.'

'Can we go out there?'

'Sure. Erm, yeah, let's go out there.' Ben turned back into the room to find Anna already in the hallway, finding her shoes and coat, pulling them on. She beckoned for him to hurry, and then she was by the back door, trying to work out how to unlock it.

Ben did it for her, reaching around to turn the key and push the door open. It went with the crack of thick snow moving and they both stood on the threshold, looking out at the cold, white garden.

'Is there anything I should be aware of? Any ponds to fall in?' Anna asked, taking the first tentative step outside.

'No ponds. No holes. No deep wells to lose you in,' said Ben, following her out. He closed the back door behind him to keep the warmth inside the house.

When he turned back, a snowball hit him hard in the chest, followed by peels of Anna's laughter.

19

Anna

Ben looked up, bewildered, and then a grin grew on his face. Anna's heart jolted at the sight and she squealed as Ben bent to make his own snowball.

She hurried to make another but had to turn away as Ben threw his ball. It exploded on her back.

'Ouch! Did I throw that hard? Come away from the window so I can throw this properly.'

'Oh! That's why your throw was so weak, huh?' cried Ben, moving away from the house, onto what Anna presumed was probably lawn when everything wasn't under such a thick layer of snow. There wasn't even a hint of a blade of grass peaking through.

Another snowball flew past her head.

'Hang on!' she cried, throwing hers and easily missing him. She hurried to make another but Ben was now ahead of her. Glancing hurriedly around, there was nowhere to hide, so Anna made herself small and gathered as much snow as her gloved fingers would allow.

When she stood, a snowball hit her in the chest.

'My boob!' she cried, the air rushing from her lungs.

She threw two snowballs in retaliation. Only one hit Ben, on his shoulder.

He laughed and approached carefully, holding up his hands.

'Hey, hey, I'm sorry. Did I hurt your boob?'

A tingle ran through Anna and she nodded, placing a hand over her right breast.

'Yes, this one.'

'Can I do anything to help?' Ben reached her, his breath coming out in a cloud, and suddenly all Anna wanted was to be enveloped in his warmth.

Instead, she gave him a wicked grin and shoved her handful of snow that had dreams of being a snowball down the inside of his coat.

Ben gave a roar of a scream, laughing as he jumped away and held his coat away from his body, snow falling from the bottom.

'Is that not what you had in mind?' Anna asked, jumping away, laughing.

'Not really.'

Another snowball hit Anna and she gave a happy squeal. She fired a snowball back but missed entirely.

'You're a bad throw,' Ben told her, advancing.

'Yeah, I'm better when you're up close,' said Anna, holding up another handful of snow threateningly.

Ben stopped, his eyes flashing as he grinned.

'Worth it,' he murmured, rushing towards her.

Anna gave a light, playful scream as she let Ben catch her, and then a proper scream as ice cold slush found its way inside the front of her coat.

'Oooh.' She pushed away from him, holding her coat away from her jumper, trying to dislodge the snow he'd shoved inside. 'Copycat,' she told him, sticking out her tongue.

Ben raised an eyebrow.

'I can be original,' he told her, forming another snowball. 'Come here.'

Anna scooped up her own handful of snow, a shiver running down the front of her body as the wind picked up.

They circled one another until, laughing, they both ran at each other, trying to fend the other off while simultaneously attempting to shove snow beneath their coats. They ended up in a tangle on the ground, the deep snow accepting them and soaking through their clothes.

Anna gave a cry as Ben managed to put some snow down her top, and he gave a yell as she shoved some ice down his back.

'You went under my clothes!' she told him breathlessly.

'So did you! Sorry, I didn't mean to,' said Ben, letting Anna go and flopping back into the snow.

Anna watched him as she tried to rub warmth into her chest, shivering. Ben glanced at her and then held out an arm. She curled up against him in the snow, her cheek against his wet coat, pressing her wet front to him.

'This doesn't really help,' she mumbled into his clothes. 'I think I'm more wet now.'

Ben laughed and kissed the top of her head.

'We should go inside and get warm,' he said against her hair.

A more pleasurable shiver ran through Anna.

'Have you ever made snow angels?' she asked, lifting her face to his.

'No. Have you?'

'No. I've only seen them in American movies. We never had enough snow.'

'Well, we do now.'

They grinned at one another and then Anna shuffled away. Slowly, watching each other, they spread out their arms and legs and moved them in and out.

'Do you think that's it?' Ben asked, breathless as he stopped.

Anna shrugged.

'Maybe?'

They stared at one another, both breathing hard.

'My chest is freezing,' Anna murmured.

Their eyes locked, Ben and Anna shuffled closer

to one another and their lips met in a haze of warmth. Anna moaned into the kiss, wishing she could press her entire body against Ben's heat. The snow was in her hair and on the side of her face as they kissed. If she gave it any thought, she would struggle to find a part of her body that was still dry.

Ben's tongue touched hers and the kiss deepened. Without thinking, just needing to be closer to his warmth, Anna hooked a leg over him, pulling him closer. Ben responded with a light sigh, his hands rummaging around her chest.

Giggling to herself, Anna stopped him and unzipped her coat just enough to give him access.

'Your jumper's soaked!'

'I did say,' said Anna, her voice low as Ben gently squeezed her breasts through the layers. Their noses bumped together and they kissed again.

She ran a hand down his wet coat until she reached his jeans, finding with joy how his body was responding to the feel of her wet jumper.

He gave a small gasp into her mouth as she gave him a little squeeze back.

'We should go inside,' she murmured.

'Oh.'

'We can't stay outside in the freezing snow,' she pointed out.

'I suppose.' Ben kissed her lips again, his thumb finding her hard nipple through the layers. Another pleasurable shiver ran through Anna.

'It's warmer inside,' she told him, kissing his

lower lip. 'We won't need all these clothes.'

Ben looked into her eyes in such a way that made her reconsider moving. They could have sex in the snow. It would be romantic and fun, wouldn't it? They didn't need to undress. She'd have to remove her trousers, she supposed – and that was an immediate no. At the very thought, a cold shiver ran up her legs, violently shaking her.

Ben frowned.

'Time to go inside.' He removed his hands and did up her coat, before pushing himself to his feet and holding out a hand to help Anna up.

Looking down at the shapes they'd made in the snow, Anna tutted.

'Well, that doesn't look like an angel. Just a hole of smush.'

Ben laughed and wrapped an arm around her.

'They probably looked amazing before you couldn't keep your hands off me.'

Anna beamed and put her arm around him.

'You're the one who wanted to open my coat.'

'And just how many times did you tell me your chest was cold? I was doing the gentlemanly thing of warming it up.'

Anna gazed up into Ben's eyes until a gust of wind rocked through them.

'Inside,' Ben declared, herding her back to the door.

They both stepped into the house and Ben shut the door behind them. The house was remarkably warmer than the garden and Anna immediately began to defrost.

They removed and shook out their coats and boots, leaving them by the door to dry. Anna padded to the oven to check on everything.

'Seems to be going well,' she said quietly, unsure of what she was looking for. She gave another shiver, hugging herself despite that meaning she was holding her wet jumper closer to her body. She looked up to find Ben watching her with a concerned frown.

'Go have another shower and get warm,' he told her. 'I'll go sort out the fire.'

'What about you? You're wet and cold too.'

'I'll have a shower after you.'

Anna hesitated, staring at Ben.

'We could have a shower together?'

Ben made a scoffing noise, which Anna tried not to take personally. She smiled and left the kitchen, climbing the stairs, checking out the hall window as she went. The view was so different without the falling snow blocking it. She could just make out the shape of her car on the road, through the heavy-laden trees. Going on tiptoe, she tried to see the state of the road. There were no tyre marks, no footprints that she could see. It was still impassable.

Smiling, Anna jogged up the rest of the stairs and went into her bedroom.

So Ben didn't want to have a shower with her.

That was all right, lots of people didn't like joint showers. Plus, someone needed to keep an eye on the turkey in the oven.

Anna pulled off her wet clothes and tried to drape them over the warm radiator. She grabbed her towel and darted across the hallway to the shower. Shivering, she hugged her naked body as she waited for the water to heat up and then she stepped in with a groan of pleasure.

She'd meant to shower quickly, but the heat made her slow so she could relish it. She stood under the shower head, letting the hot water run through her cold, wet hair, and closed her eyes.

A smile grew as she replayed the snowball fight in the garden. Ben's grin, his playful laugh, the feel of his hands on her, albeit pushing snow down her coat and then down her top.

Anna opened her eyes, her body tingling and not just from the warmth of the shower.

She rubbed shower gel into her arms to clean off any remaining dirt and snow, and tried hard to push the idea of Ben's hands on her wet, naked body from her head. With a sigh, she washed the rest of her body, just in case. Her fingers lingered over her breasts as she remembered Ben's words, his voice developing a husky edge. For a moment, she pretended her fingers were his and closed her eyes. She exhaled slowly as she ran her fingers down to her thighs.

Anna opened her eyes and removed her hands.

She couldn't do this. In a sudden moment of realisation, she found herself in the bathroom of a man she'd known for two days, naked, alone and acting as if she'd known him for years. Biting her lip, she stood under the hot water and let the soap wash away.

It did feel like years, and yet when she thought about it, she knew so little about Ben. Other than what he did for a living, where his family were, how he'd come about this house. Anna frowned. She even knew why his marriage had failed.

She knew him enough.

Her fingers trailed back between her legs, but she stopped herself again. She wasn't the only one who had been shivering when they'd come back into the house, and she didn't want to use up all the hot water. That wasn't a problem for her back home, but she got the impression it was something that could happen in this old house.

If she could stay, that would be the first thing she'd change.

Anna turned off the water, squeezed out her hair and reached for the towel. As she reached, her foot slipped and she threw out an arm to stop herself from falling. The shower gel and shampoo bottles clattered to her feet.

Steadying herself, Anna carefully scooped up the bottles and purposefully stepped out of the shower, wrapping the towel around her, heart pounding from what could have been.

20

Ben

As Anna had made her way up the stairs, Ben had watched, only turning away when she was out of sight. What was he thinking? Checking on the oven and finding nothing amiss, Ben sat on a chair at the kitchen table and put his head in his damp hands.

He hardly knew this woman. Sitting up, Ben counted on his fingers the facts he knew about her. That her parents were divorced, that her ex-boyfriend Brad wanted her back and was pretty insistent – Ben didn't like that – that she'd lost her job and didn't know what she wanted now. He sat back and sighed, rubbing his cold fingers over his defrosting face. Being around Anna was so easy, as if she'd always been here.

He looked up at the kitchen ceiling and silently asked his uncle if this was the right thing. Not that his uncle would answer. Ben knew what he'd say if he was still around: follow your heart, Ben.

Nibbling on his lower lip, Ben sat forward and tried to figure out what he wanted. He should have been having those thoughts while making a fire. The house's heating wasn't penetrating his wet clothes fast enough, but Ben's legs wouldn't move.

He wanted Anna.

He couldn't explain why, but his whole body seemed to be shouting at him. Not to go upstairs, not to seek her out, but to make sure she was warm and safe, to make her smile, to keep her in his life for as long as she wanted to be around.

Ben gave a violent shiver, the chill from his wet clothes seeping further into him. Standing, he slowly moved towards the living room and the open fireplace, when there came a loud crash from above his head.

He didn't think. Rushing up the stairs, taking them two at a time, Ben found himself out of breath by Anna's bathroom door.

'Anna? Are you okay?'

'I'm fine!' came Anna's voice. 'Sorry! I just dropped a couple of bottles. Everything's fine.'

'Okay. You're sure? That was a loud bang.'

'I did almost fall.' Anna's voice was quieter and Ben held his breath for a moment.

'Did you just say you almost fell?'

There was a pause, too long for Ben's liking, and then, 'Yeah. But I'm okay. Just a little slip.'

'Did you fall?'

'No, I knocked two bottles over.'

Ben would have laughed if he had the breath. He leaned against the wall and placed a hand on his chest to calm his beating heart, closing his eyes.

He opened them at the sound of the bathroom door opening and Anna's voice.

'Oops!'

Ben turned to the door where Anna was emerging, her long hair wet, her towel dropped to her waist.

He looked away hurriedly, staring down the hallway, concentrating on his bedroom door at the far end.

'Are you all right?' he asked, keeping his eyes from her.

'Yeah. I thought I'd fastened the towel, but obviously not. Sorry about that. Are you okay?'

'Yeah... Is it safe?' Ben asked carefully.

'I don't think my breasts can hurt you.'

Slowly, Ben turned back, half-expecting, half-hoping that the towel would still be dropped. It wasn't. The towel was wrapped around Anna's body, covering her, but her smile suggested she could drop it again at any time.

'Sorry,' he murmured. 'I didn't see anything.'

Anna gave him a funny look.

'Of course you did. And you've seen them before,' she reminded him, glancing back into the bathroom. 'Sorry I scared you.' She stepped back inside, hanging up the bathmat to dry.

'Yeah, but that's when you wanted me to see them.' Ben followed her with his eyes, looking around the bathroom. 'Well, I'm glad you're okay.'

'And I appreciate you running up the stairs like that.' Anna gave him a sweet smile, making his stomach twist pleasurably. 'Is the turkey okay?'

It took Ben a moment to realise what she was talking about.

'Oh. Yes, everything's going well.'

'Touch wood.' Anna looked around the bathroom quickly and then touched her own head.

Ben cleared his throat.

'Fine. So far, everything's going well.'

Anna flashed him a grin.

'That's better. I'm sure the moment I step in the kitchen, something will burn.' Having tidied and opened the window to let out the steam, Anna approached Ben. He moved out of the way and she wandered to her bedroom, but she didn't shut the door. Ben's feet refused to move. 'Have you lit the fire? Did I interrupt it?' Anna asked.

'Oh. No. I haven't started yet.' Ben's feet shuffled a little, but still, he didn't move.

After a moment, Anna sat on the foot of her bed, still only wearing a towel, and patted the space beside her.

Mouth dry, Ben wandered into the room and went to sit next to her before remembering himself.

'I'm still wet,' he said, patting his damp clothes.

'Oh, right. You should go have a shower. Get warm. I feel a lot better.'

Ben stared into Anna's large, beautiful eyes.

'I should...give you some privacy. To get dressed and stuff. Before you get cold.' He edged back towards the door and took great delight in watching Anna's expression fall a little.

She glanced out of the window.

'I suppose I should pack my bag,' she murmured. 'As the snow's stopped.'

Ben froze.

'Oh.'

Anna snapped round to look at him.

'Oh?'

'Well, yeah, I suppose,' Ben said with a struggle, his frown returning. It was only as the creases appeared between his eyes that he realised it had been a while since he'd properly frowned. It even hurt a little. 'You'll want to get to that cottage.'

'After Christmas dinner.'

Ben's frown eased.

'Good! Not sure I could eat everything you've prepared by myself.'

They stared at one another, smiling, neither moving.

'I'll, erm, go have a shower, then,' Ben said slowly.

'Don't worry, I won't have a go at lighting the fire,' Anna told him, grinning mercilessly.

Ben barked a short laugh, turned to leave and

changed his mind, glancing back to that spot next to Anna on the bed. She patted it again.

'You can sit for a minute,' she offered quietly. 'Unless you're really cold?'

Ben shook his head.

'Aren't you getting cold?' He stepped towards the bed, blinking at the voices arguing in his head. If he sat down, they would both get cold. Unless they ended up underneath the covers. Images of what lay beneath Anna's towel flashed before him.

'No,' said Anna gently, patting the spot beside her again. 'Come sit down.'

Relieved, Ben did as he was told, perching beside her, aware of not wanting to make her bed damp from his clothes. Her fingers brushed against his.

'Oh, you are cold.' Anna picked up his hand between hers and rubbed them together.

He gave her a curious look.

'Are you trying to warm up just one hand?' he asked, realising what he was saying as it fell out of his mouth.

Anna stopped.

'Well, yeah, here, give me your other hand, I'll warm that one too.'

Ben raised an eyebrow and Anna laughed, leaning towards him. She stopped when he hesitated.

'Have I misread the situation?' she whispered.

Ben shook his head.

'I don't think so.'

'You don't want to kiss me?'

Ben exhaled with a shiver.

'I do.' His gaze moved down to her lips and then to the hem of her towel, pressing against her bare, warm skin that had to be growing colder by the second.

'Do you want to do more than just kiss?' came Anna's soft voice.

He met her eyes and nodded.

'Do you?'

She gave an eager nod, and then her warm lips were on his. Her hands were on his cheeks, and before he could grasp what was happening, Anna was up, swinging a leg over him and straddling him. He put his hands on her waist, over the towel, as they kissed, being careful not to touch her skin with his cold fingers.

Anna's hands were gentle on his cheeks, running down to his neck, fingers sliding down his chest, over his jumper. She leaned back a little, letting her towel fall to her waist, and Ben caught a glimpse of her breasts before she pulled his jumper off over his head.

'Is this okay?' she asked.

Ben nodded, ripping his gaze back up to her eyes.

Laughing, Anna kissed him again, harder this time, until Ben pushed her gently away. He removed his damp t-shirt and it was Anna's turn to stare at his chest. Smiling, she ran her fingers over his skin and light chest hair.

'Oh, you're warm.' Her dancing eyes lifted to his.

'I thought you'd be freezing and wet after all that snow I shoved down here.'

Ben laughed.

'I think the sight of you warmed me up,' he told her, brushing his lips over hers and then moving to plant kisses down her neck to her collarbone.

Anna shivered in his arms.

'Are you cold?' he murmured between kisses.

'Not anymore.' The words came as a breath in his ear, spurring him on.

Anna lifted herself as he kissed below her collarbone, working his way down.

A loud roaring sound filled the room and Anna jerked away.

'What's that?'

Glancing around, she held him tightly, using him to cover herself.

Ben tried to orient himself, his lips had been so close to her nipple, at that moment he wasn't even sure what room he was in. The noise became louder, finally breaking through his thoughts, and he looked to the window.

'Sounds like a tractor, maybe trying to get through the snow.' He turned back to Anna, desperate for her lips on his.

Anna climbed off him, wrapping the towel about her and moved to the window.

'You're right. A tractor is ploughing the snow. I hope my car isn't in the way.'

Not willing to stand up at that moment, Ben

watched from the bed.

'It's probably the farmer up the road. He'll know to come knock if it is in the way.' His gaze moved down her body, his mind whirring with ideas of how to get her back on that bed with him.

Anna sighed deeply and turned to Ben.

'Is that the turkey I can smell?'

Ben took a deep breath and nodded. He sighed.

'Should I let you get dressed?'

Anna bit her lower lip and it was all Ben could do not to rush over and scoop her into his arms.

'I suppose so.' Anna hugged herself and glanced out of the window again.

Ben stood and made his way to the door.

'I'll go check on the turkey before I have a shower,' he said, all of the sudden warmth and excitement gone from his body. He closed the bedroom door behind him and walked slowly down the stairs, a cold shiver setting in as he reached the warmth of the kitchen.

21

Anna

Why hadn't she told Ben to stay put? Anna wasn't sure. She'd been getting cold wearing only a towel, but that hadn't been anything Ben and a duvet couldn't have fixed. Now he was back downstairs, the door closed, and the road had been ploughed.

She could leave.

Once she got her car working, or someone to give her a lift. Ben could even give her a lift, now that he could get his car on the road.

Anna gave a heavy sigh and dropped her towel, reaching for clean, dry clothes. She didn't have to think about that yet. First there would be Christmas dinner. She did her best to push it all from her head and delved into her bag looking for a clean pair of socks.

Anna jumped, her heart squeezing, as a loud

beeping sounded through the house. Pausing to listen, she grabbed her socks and pulled them on. It was the smoke alarm.

She was still pulling her dress down over her hips as she threw open her bedroom door and ran down the stairs, despite the beeping having stopped.

'What's happening? Is everything okay?'

Ben was in the kitchen, waving a kitchen towel at the smoke alarm on the ceiling, the back door wide open. A gust of freezing wind blew in and under Anna's dress. She gave a shiver, remembering the thick jumper she'd left on her bed, and checked the worktops for signs of anything burning. 'What happened?' she repeated. 'Did I burn something?'

Ben gave a half frown and shook his head.

'How? You weren't here.'

'Well, I... No, I guess not.'

'It's nothing.'

'Is the food burned?' Anna strode to the oven to check the turkey.

'No.'

'Then what set it off?'

When she turned to Ben, she found him with rosy cheeks, looking anywhere but at her. Anna checked her dress, to make sure he wasn't just being polite. No, she was covered and fully clothed. She glanced back to him. 'I know that look,' she murmured, approaching him. 'What did you do?' She moved until he was forced to meet her gaze, and then she raised a questioning eyebrow, a smile playing on her lips.

Ben relented with a sigh.

'I thought it would be nice...to light some candles,' he admitted, pointing to the kitchen table where he'd laid out placemats, cutlery and some candles.

'Aw, that is nice,' said Anna. 'Of course that's nice. It didn't go well?'

Ben pursed his lips.

'I may have set fire to a napkin.' He gestured to a scorched linen napkin in the sink.

Anna burst out laughing and smacked a hand over her mouth to stop herself.

'I'm sorry. That's not funny.'

When she looked back to Ben, she caught him watching her with soft eyes. 'It really is a nice thought,' she added gently.

'Romantic,' he murmured, barely audible. 'I thought it would be romantic.'

A heat spread through Anna, her heart squeezing, her body responding to an instant memory of Ben's lips on her skin.

'All of this is romantic,' she admitted, a little breathless.

His soft eyes became keen, watching her take a step closer.

'See, it's not just you that bad, silly things happen to,' he said, his voice huskier than it had been only seconds ago.

Anna wet her lips.

'No, maybe I'm rubbing off on you.'

Ben's gaze drifted down to her dress, noticing it for the first time.

'You look amazing.'

Another freezing gust of wind blew in through the open door, lifting her skirt and sending a shiver through her.

'Ooh, thank you. We can close this now, right?' She went to close the back door before he could agree. 'You must be freezing with that wind, and you still haven't showered or changed.'

Ben appeared to wake up.

'Right. Yeah. I'll go and, erm, shower.'

'Want some company?'

Ben stopped and looked back to Anna.

'You just had a shower.'

She shrugged and gave him what she hoped was a playful smile. 'I don't mind. Although, I think we should both be aware that if I am rubbing off on you, we should be extra careful in a slippery shower.'

Ben grinned and Anna's heart pounded at the sight.

'To be fair,' she added, approaching him slowly, 'maybe my bad luck isn't catching.'

Ben's gaze drifted down her again.

'Maybe I distract you?' she accidentally asked; she hadn't meant for the question mark to go on the end of that sentence. Anna gently cleared her throat and lifted her chin.

'You do have incredible breasts,' he murmured.

Anna blinked and met Ben's eyes, but he turned away, his cheeks rosier than before.

'I'm going to shower,' he announced.

'Well, wait, hang on.' Anna went to follow him but looked back to the oven. 'What stage are we at? What needs doing?'

'The turkey is still cooking. We're about an hour off putting the potatoes on. I think,' said Ben, frowning at he worked out the timings.

Anna closed the distance between them and slid her hand into his. Reaching up, she smoothed out the frown lines between his eyes and then hooked a finger under the collar of his jumper, guiding him down until she could kiss him.

Ben broke the kiss and searched her eyes.

'I'm going to have a shower,' he told her gently. 'If you happen to be on my bed when I come out, then that's up to you.'

Anna grinned.

'On or in?'

Ben's gaze drifted down to where her dress hugged her waist

'Again, up to you.'

He planted a soft kiss on her lips and then let go of her hand, jogging up the stairs and disappearing.

Anna watched him go, her entire body already tingling with anticipation. She glanced over the cooking food, tried to concentrate and ensure everything was safe, and then she slowly made her way up the stairs.

Halfway up, she heard her phone, still in her bedroom, beep with an incoming message. Sighing, listening to the shower running in Ben's en suite, she diverted to her room to check the message.

Merry Christmas, my lovely Anna. Are you all right?

It was from her mother. Smiling, Anna typed out a reply.

Merry Christmas, Mum. I'm great. Best Christmas I could hope for away from family. I'm sorry about earlier. I really am happy and having a great Christmas. I hope you are too. See you next week.

She hit send and then pulled off her dress and socks, padding barefoot through the hallway, she sat on Ben's impeccably made bed and waited for him. It didn't take long for her to get cold and she eyed the duvet. Slipping underneath, she took deep breaths of Ben's scent in the cotton duvet cover while she waited, sitting in his bed wearing only her underwear, his duvet pulled up to her chin.

Soon after, the shower switched off. A couple of minutes later, the bathroom door opened and Ben glanced out. His eyes lit up as he spotted her and

Anna grinned, waving at him.

She pulled the duvet down, moving into the middle of the bed.

With a smile, Ben opened the door to reveal his damp body, a towel wrapped around his waist.

'I wasn't sure you'd be here,' he said, sitting beside her.

'Of course. You want me here, right?'

Ben nodded.

'Pretty much all I could think about in the shower.' He leaned over and kissed her.

Anna wrapped her arms around him, pulling him closer. Then she broke the kiss and took off her bra. Ben watched, his lips twitching.

'Maybe we should get under the duvet,' she suggested.

'You're cold?'

Anna nodded. Ben pulled the duvet over them and wrapped an arm around her waist. He pulled her to him, pressing himself against her and Anna let out a moan.

'You're so warm!'

His lips were on her neck and then shoulder, working over to her collarbone and then down her chest to her breasts. Anna flopped back, giving him full access, and closed her eyes to relish the feel of his lips on her.

It didn't take long for her breathing to become heavy. She gently pushed him away and pulled off her underwear, giving the towel still at his waist a little tug. He removed the towel, throwing it across the room and they cautiously gazed over each other's bodies beneath the duvet.

Grinning, Anna met his eyes and they were kissing again. Deep, hungry kisses that left Anna both weak and in need of more at the same time. She ran her hands down Ben's chest to his groin and, to her delight, Ben did the same, running his hand down to her hip and then between her legs.

There was a part of Anna that had wanted things to hurry along, longing for the feel of Ben inside her, for that release. Ben, however, had other ideas.

Just as Anna was going to ask about the possibility or existence of protection, Ben eased down her body, placing kisses as he went. The air rushed out of Anna's lungs and Ben lifted his head to check with her. Silently, she nodded emphatically and Ben went back to what he was doing. Anna looked down at Ben's head between her legs as his tongue explored her. She pushed the fingers of one hand through his hair, raising her other arm over her head to grasp at the pillow.

He didn't raise his head again until she'd finished writhing on his bed, filling the house with her moans, and she gently pushed him away and beckoned him back up to her lips.

'Do you have any protection?' she asked, kissing his lower lip.

'Somewhere,' he breathed, reaching for the bedside table. He brought out a box and Anna raised her eyebrows.

'You just have that ready and waiting?'

'To be honest, they've been here a while.' Ben sat up. 'Do they have a use by date?'

'Probably,' said Anna, pulling herself up and placing kisses on his chest.

Ben checked the box, turning it over and over in his hands.

'This is hard to do when you're doing that,' he murmured.

'You want me to stop?' Anna asked, gripping him in one hand.

Ben gave a soft moan and tore open the box.

22

Ben

They'd gone through two condoms when Ben, breathing hard, lying on his back with the duvet entangled around his legs and Anna curled up against his chest, remembered the Christmas dinner in the oven downstairs.

The idea of the turkey burning wasn't enough to make his legs move, or even make his voice work. He continued silently stroking Anna's waist and hip, running his fingers over her, memorising every curve. Who needed Christmas dinner when he was in bed with the most glorious woman?

Smiling to himself, Ben imagined what could be. Could this become a Christmas tradition? Sex while the dinner cooked. Not if they had children, of course. But before then, on Christmas Day morning. On Christmas Eve morning. On any morning,

Ben thought. Sex with Anna every morning, if they could. That's what he wanted.

'Do you like morning sex?' he asked, his lips in her hair as he kissed the top of her head.

'Sometimes,' came her muffled voice against his chest. 'Do you?'

'Yeah. When do you prefer it?'

'Just on Christmas Day.'

Ben stopped, blinking up at the ceiling.

Anna lifted her head and grinned at him.

'You just held your breath,' she told him. 'I was joking.' She kissed his chest and then his neck, working her way up to his lips. 'I like Boxing Day sex, too.'

Ben laughed and kissed her hard, gently pushing her until he lay over her. She wrapped her legs around him, pulling him in, when he remembered his original thought.

'The potatoes need putting in,' he said between kisses on her neck.

'Yeah, they do,' said Anna with a giggle.

'No.' Ben lifted his head, smiling, kissing Anna's lips again. 'The roast potatoes. Downstairs.'

'Oh.' Anna's smile fell, replaced with an expression of serious realisation. 'I completely forgot.'

'Glad I could have that effect on you,' said Ben, trying his luck, dipping his mouth down to her breasts.

Anna lay back, stroking his head.

'So... We should go put the potatoes on?'

'At least one of us should,' said Ben around her nipple.

There was silence as Ben played with her breasts and Anna watched him, her legs already squirming, pulling him closer. He resisted, using every inch of willpower to pull himself away from her. 'I'll go put the potatoes in. Don't want you rushing and having an accident.'

Anna laughed and stretched her arms above her head.

'Fair enough. Be careful but be quick.'

Ben climbed off the bed and took a good look at Anna's naked body. He grabbed the towel from the floor and wrapped it about his waist as he ran down the stairs to the kitchen. Putting the potatoes on to boil, he checked everything else, and then ran back up the stairs.

'We have about ten minutes before I need to put the potatoes in the oven,' he declared as he walked back into his bedroom.

He stopped. His bed was empty.

Looking around, his chest tightened a little, and then came the sound of the toilet in his en suite flushing. Anna stepped out of the bathroom and rushed to him, wrapping herself about him.

'It's freezing out here,' she told him.

Ben laughed and scooped her up, placing her back on the bed.

'Did you hear what I said?'

'I did. What can we do in ten minutes?' Anna

asked playfully, kneeling up and pushing at the towel. It fell to the floor and Ben couldn't move. He stood still, watching Anna, stroking her hair, his toes curling on the cold, wooden floorboards.

Ben made his way back down the stairs, a little weak at the knees, to put the parboiled potatoes into the oven to roast. Checking everything was going well, he dashed back up the stairs.

'Twenty minutes,' he announced.

Anna made room for him in the bed and he slid beneath the duvet, snaking his arms around her, his lips finding her neck. Ben didn't think he would ever get tired of Anna wrapping her legs around him, pulling him close. It had fast become his new favourite thing.

Perhaps not his absolute new favourite thing, if he was honest. That came after. First, he enjoyed kissing and stroking Anna's body, taking note of which places made her squirm with pleasure, at what points she let out a sharp exhale. It had been so long since Ben had been in bed with a woman, but it felt as if he'd always been in bed with Anna. She seemed to already know his body so well, he could make her back arch with a single touch, their bodies synced easily as he slid inside her.

Before they knew what had happened, ten minutes had passed and they lay side by side, Ben trying to catch his breath as Anna entwined her fingers in his and kissed his shoulder.

'Should we wash before we eat? We probably should,' she said between kisses. 'That'll take longer than five minutes. Right?'

'We could share a shower,' Ben suggested.

'I thought the house couldn't take that, or whatever?'

Ben laughed and rolled on to his side to face her, his hand lying on her hip.

'It can't take both showers on at the same time. It can take one shower with two people.'

Anna scoffed and bumped her nose against his.

'I'm pretty sure I suggested that ages ago.'

'Yeah, but you were cold and covered in snow. You'd say anything in that situation, and I didn't want to take advantage.'

Anna laughed and kissed him. When they parted, he studied her, taking in every feature and committing it to memory. She searched his eyes.

'Did I take advantage of you?' she murmured.

'Absolutely not.'

'Has this been amazing for you too?' she asked, her voice even quieter.

Ben nodded.

'The best,' he whispered, brushing his thumb over her lower lip.

They stared into one another's eyes for a moment, the same words repeating in Ben's mind, over and over.

Don't go. Don't go. Don't go.

'Everything's probably burning now,' Anna

whispered.

'And we haven't even put the veg on.'

'Oh no!' said Anna, moving to sit up.

Ben watched her as the duvet fell from her body.

'You go put the veg on,' he told her, sitting up and kissing her neck. 'I'll go start the fire and get the house warm.'

Grinning, Anna agreed, kissing his lips and slipping out of the bed. There was a slow hunt for their clothes and then they wandered downstairs, aware that they should be hurrying but simply not capable of it.

Anna went into the kitchen while Ben parted with her, going into the living room and kneeling in front of the fireplace. It needed cleaning first and Ben inwardly cursed himself. His uncle had always cleaned the fireplace the morning after the fire, laying it ready for that night. Ben had always done the same, but that morning it had slipped his mind. A grin broke out on his face and he shook it away, leaving a contented smile in its place.

The fire was crackling and settling when Anna called Ben in to help her dish up the Christmas dinner. She'd lit the candles on the kitchen table and the scorched napkin was nowhere to be seen, presumably hidden in the bin. The food was mostly in serving bowls on the worktop, so they could help themselves, but the turkey sat resting on the top of the oven.

'Can you carve?' Anna asked.

Ben nodded and found the knives, setting to work, placing thin pieces of turkey on their plates. Then they piled them high with roast potatoes and carrots, parsnips, broccoli and cabbage. Ben helped himself to cranberry sauce, but Anna pulled a face at it. As Ben sat at the table, Anna made a strange noise and reached for the oven gloves.

'Almost forgot the pigs in blankets. Can you imagine?'

She pulled out the tray and slid the pigs in blankets into a bowl, turning to take them to the table. Despite there being nothing on the floor, she somehow tripped, the bowl of food lifting in the air.

Ben stood and reached out, catching her and the bowl just before she fell and everything spilled.

Eyes wide, Anna looked up at Ben.

'You keep falling into my arms,' he murmured.

Anna melted into him a little.

'Best habit I've ever had,' she told him.

His touch lingered, he didn't want to let go of her, but the smell of the food was too much. They'd worked up enough of an appetite. Ben sat and Anna put the bowl on the table. They helped themselves to the pigs in blankets and gravy, and Ben poured wine into their glasses.

'This is incredible,' said Ben around a mouthful. 'I haven't had Christmas dinner like this in years.'

'What do you normally have?'

Ben shrugged.

'Maybe a turkey and cranberry sandwich or

something.'

'A sandwich!'

'In front of the TV.'

'Let me guess, and then back to work?'

Ben grimaced.

'To be fair, I didn't have much else to do.'

Anna sighed.

'Not even any friends around here to visit?'

'They're all in London, what's left of them,' Ben admitted. 'I like being here alone. I liked being here alone,' he corrected himself, glancing up at her. 'Now I like having you here.' He looked back to his food, blinking, his mouth dry as he waited for her reaction.

'Well, I'm something for you to do.'

Ben laughed and reached for his wine.

'I think it's more than sex,' he said without thinking. Freezing, he glanced back to her. Anna was smiling to herself, piling her fork high.

'Good,' she murmured. 'I think so too. At least, I hope so. You don't think all those interruptions meant something?' She looked away hurriedly, shoving the forkful of food into her mouth.

Ben gave this some thought.

'No. If they had, we would have been interrupted again. And again, and again. Wouldn't we?' He couldn't help the boyish grin as Anna looked up to meet his eyes. 'Maybe something didn't want us getting together until Christmas Day.' He gave a small shrug and then realised what he'd said. When he lifted his gaze to check on Anna, she was smiling at him, her eyes soft.

They went back to their meals.

'It's so quiet here,' said Anna. 'I just thought it was quiet because it was snowing.'

'The snow will still be muffling everything. But it is usually quiet here. We don't get much traffic other than tractors and villagers and the odd woman breaking down during a snowstorm.'

'As in a woman every now and then, or are you calling me an odd woman?'

Ben smiled.

'Both.' He winked at her and his stomach warmed in pleasure at she gave a happy wriggle in her seat, reaching for her wine. It was a similar movement to the one she made when his tongue was between her legs.

Ben cleared his throat and reached for his own drink.

'I've never lived somewhere so quiet,' said Anna, unaware of Ben's thoughts. 'I grew up in the middle of a town, then lived in the city. Maybe it's time for some countryside living. What jobs can I do in the country? Farm labourer?'

Ben frowned.

'You could work in a coffee shop. Lots of independent coffee shops in these villages, we get quite a few tourists in the summer.'

'I bet. Oh, I'd like that. Working in a coffee shop, or tea shop, meeting new people. I used to be a waitress and apart from getting slapped on the bum every now and then by some drunken idiot, it was a great job. Maybe I need to go back to that. And I reckon you get fewer drunk idiots in quaint village tea shops.'

Ben chewed thoughtfully.

'Maybe you could look for those jobs in the new year,' he suggested.

'Hmm. I'm not sure I could get by, they don't pay enough, not if you're living alone.'

Ben smiled, watching her eat.

'Yeah. True,' he murmured, thinking back to how beautiful she'd made the living room.

'Maybe I could open my own tea shop. Then I'd be working so hard I wouldn't need a home, because I could just sleep there.' Anna laughed to herself.

Ben was about say, 'Or you could stay here,' but he stopped himself, and then the words vanished, lost in his throat as he watched her eat, before remembering his own food was getting cold.

23

Anna

With the dinner eaten, Anna shooed Ben into the warm living room to check on the fire and relax while she tidied up. A smile was apparently permanently plastered to her face; she just couldn't remove it.

All in all, this was shaping up to be the best Christmas since her childhood. A beautiful house, a gorgeous man, amazing sex, great food, a plan for the new year and nothing had gone wrong.

Anna opened the microwave so she would remember to wipe it down and found a bowl of defrosting peas inside.

'Oh, for the love of—'

Sighing, she took the bowl out and laughed, taking it into the living room to show Ben.

'I forgot the peas!' she announced.

He was sitting back on the sofa, one hand on his stomach, the other holding the TV remote. 'I just found them in the microwave, ready to go.'

Looking over, Ben laughed and reached out for her. He pulled her onto his lap and kissed her.

'As much as I love this, my stomach can't take it,' she murmured, kissing him again.

'That's fine. As much as I love this, it was a mistake, if you stay there I might throw up,' Ben whispered.

Laughing, Anna climbed off him, taking care not to spill any peas, and then she stopped.

'We both love that, huh?' She flashed Ben a grin and walked out of the room before he could answer.

She was staring at the dishwasher when Ben appeared at the doorway.

'I can't let you do all the tidying up,' he told her.

'No, no. I'm your guest and I'm indebted and—'

'I think we're past that,' he told her, taking over and filling the dishwasher. 'Plus, if I help, it'll be done quicker and we can both sit down.'

Anna's heavy stomach gurgled.

'True. All right. Thank you.'

Ben shook his head.

'Thank you. For all of this.'

'Technically you did the cooking,' Anna pointed out. 'Technically you multi-tasked. I was very impressed.'

Ben smiled.

'That was my aim. Throughout the whole thing.'

Anna resisted the urge to hug him. They finished tidying the kitchen, chatting about whether they had room for pudding and deciding against it, wondering what was on TV, not that Anna cared, as long as she was next to Ben.

They both fell onto the sofa with a huff and a groan. Anna glanced around, wondering where her phone was. This was the longest she'd gone without it by her side. It had to be upstairs, still waiting on her bed. It could keep waiting. She was hardly going to spend time staring at the screen when she had Ben beside her.

'I've eaten way too much,' Ben decided. 'Especially considering what I was hoping would happen after.'

Anna eyed him sideways.

'Really? Aren't you getting a little sore?'

Ben turned to her.

'No. Are you?' His frown reappeared, creating concerned lines in his face. Anna softened at the sight of them, stroking them away with her thumb.

'A little,' she admitted. 'But nothing a quick rest won't solve.' She shuffled closer and Ben put an arm around her. 'What's on TV?'

'The Snowman,' said Ben, flicking through the channels. 'Indiana Jones. We missed the King's speech.'

'The film or the actual King's speech?'

'Both,' said Ben, landing on a Christmas episode of the Great British Bake Off and putting down the remote. His fingers stroked Anna's shoulder where his hand rested just above her on the back of the sofa. She snuggled further into him and lifted her chin.

He kissed her lips.

'You taste good,' he breathed.

'Like Christmas dinner?' Anna pulled a face and went to move away but Ben stopped her.

'No. You just taste good every time I kiss you.'

Anna had to stop herself from throwing her legs over him and pulling his jumper over his head. Instead, she kissed him gently. He let out a soft moan and drew her closer. Her leg moved over his and he held it there, running his hand up and down her thigh as they kissed slowly and gently.

Anna hesitated, stopping a question from falling automatically from her mouth.

'What?' Ben asked, leaning back a little to look at her properly. 'You want to stop?'

'No,' said Anna. 'It's just... No.' She kissed him again and Ben stopped her.

'No, what? What happened then?'

Anna sighed.

'If I tell you, I'll kill the mood and you won't want to kiss me anymore. And I really like kissing you.' Her eyes dropped down his body. 'Among other things.'

She supposed he was trying not to grin, because it came out as a lopsided smile.

'You realise you have to tell me now.'

'Right,' said Anna slowly. 'Because I've sort of just killed the mood, haven't I.' She gave a frustrated moan and pulled away from Ben, sitting back against the sofa. 'Fine. It's just... Isn't this a little strange? How natural it all feels? How well do we really know each other?'

That frown reappeared on Ben's features and Anna realised with a start just how fond she was becoming of it.

'I think we know a lot about each other.' Ben shifted his position, sitting taller, facing her. 'I know it's only been a few days, or whatever, but most people would have spent a few hours together over a few days. We've spent three actual days together. We know about each other's families, what we do for a living. You know about my past marriage, I know about your ex.' Ben grumbled a little, reaching for his glass of wine on the coffee table. Anna watched him sip, smiling to herself.

'Okay, so we know about each other's pasts,' Anna agreed. 'And where we both came from, our families and things. What about the future? Is this all you want? Is this a casual thing?'

Ben blinked and put his glass back on the table. 'Oh.'

Anna shook herself.

'Sorry! We don't need to talk about those things. It doesn't matter. You're absolutely right. We know each other enough. Let's go back to kissing and enjoying Christmas.' Anna leaned towards him, but

Ben didn't reciprocate.

'No, you're right. We've done the past. We should do the future.'

'Nope! We've done the future,' said Anna quickly. 'You're looking for a new job, so am I. Done, dusted.' She went to kiss him and Ben stopped her.

'Do you want this to be a casual thing?' he asked quietly.

Anna opened and closed her mouth, her mind whirring. What was she supposed to say to that? The truth? It had been three days and she'd brought up the future. This was all her fault. They should have been kissing on the sofa all evening until the fullness in their bellies went down. This Christmas could have been all about sex. That would have been something different. She could have left this place content in the knowledge that she'd never have a Christmas quite like it again.

Anna's expression fell before she could stop it and Ben's eyes widened.

'What happened there? What did you think?' he demanded.

She shook her head.

'Nothing.'

'No, come on. Please. Anything you tell me is probably not as bad as what I'll make up.'

Anna lifted her gaze to his and laughed.

'That's usually what I say.'

Ben shrugged but said nothing, waiting for her to

confess her thoughts.

'It just occurred to me that I should be happy to just have this Christmas, because I'll probably never have a Christmas like this one again. With you. And that made me sad.'

Her stomach flipped as Ben's eyes lit up. Surely she'd just said enough to firmly scare him away.

'I've been thinking the same,' he admitted quietly.

Anna clenched her mouth shut to stop herself from yelling in surprise.

'Really?' she whispered.

'Really,' Ben said, giving her a strange look. 'You weren't expecting that?'

'Well, no.' Anna shrugged. 'For all I knew, you wanted this to be a casual thing. You know, you brought me in out of the snow, we fell into bed, and that's it.'

'Is that what you want?' Ben asked carefully.

Anna blew out her cheeks. There was a strong feeling here that they were going round in circles. She sat up properly and faced him, looking him right in the eye.

'Okay, let's be completely honest with each other. Okay? Even if we're not on the same page, that doesn't mean we can't finish a great Christmas Day together. Right? So, full honesty.'

Ben mirrored her position and nodded.

'Agreed.'

There was a pause.

'You go first,' said Ben.

'Fine. Okay. Here we go.' She cleared her throat. 'I really like you and am having a great time and maybe it would be good if this wasn't a casual thing, unless you really want it to be,' she said, the words cascading out so fast that Ben had to lean back to take them in.

'Okay,' he started. 'I really like you too and I don't think I want this to be casual either.'

'You don't think?'

Ben studied her and Anna wilted a little under the pressure of what was surely going on in his mind.

'Do you want to get married one day?' he asked hesitantly. 'Have children? I think that's more what I meant when I said talking about the future. Where do you want to be?'

Anna's stomach couldn't cope with the straight position she'd chosen. She shifted so she could lean back and relax her belly.

'Married,' said Anna. 'The older I get, the less I think marriage is important, but I would still like it. And children. One, maybe two. And a fulfilling job. And a gorgeous man who loves me.'

'He's who you want to be married to, right?' said Ben with a playful smile.

'Of course!' Anna laughed. 'What about you? Have your past experiences put you off all that?'

'No. I always wanted to be a dad,' Ben told her. 'I guess I just assumed it wouldn't happen after all that.' He stared past her for a moment. 'I would do it all again, with the right person this time. Yeah, marriage, kids, a fulfilling job and a beautiful woman who loves me. Sounds perfect.'

Anna grinned, reaching out to him. Ben took her hand, entwining his fingers with hers.

'And what about us?' she asked softly.

'Well, you're beautiful. I'd say that's a good start.'

They leaned forward at the same time and kissed.

'How full are you feeling?' she asked breathlessly.

'Not as full as I did,' said Ben, pulling her closer. 'You?'

'Same. If I climb on you now, will you throw up on me?'

Ben laughed.

'That's still a risk,' he admitted. He moved her until she was snuggled against him and then he relaxed into kissing her lips. 'We could stay here for a bit.'

'Here is good.' Anna wrapped her arms around him. Snuggling against him, kissing on the sofa, in front of the fire and TV might even be better than the sex she'd had in mind.

24
Ben

At six o'clock, Ben woke and took a moment to remember what day it was and whether he had to get up. Cursing his inner clock, he rolled over to find Anna beside him, naked and sleeping peacefully. Smiling so hard his cheeks hurt, Ben watched her as the events of Christmas night came back to him.

The kissing on the sofa had eventually led to sex on the sofa. Anna had offered to climb on top, but they were both still so full. They'd ended up lying beside one another on the sofa, Ben clinging to her so she didn't roll off the side. He hadn't laughed that much in a long time; no wonder his cheeks hurt.

They'd stayed snuggled on the sofa, stripped of most clothes, until the fire had died and the cold of the night had begun to creep over them. Anna had followed him upstairs and accepted the invitation into his bed where they'd enjoyed and explored one another for Ben didn't know how long. Long enough that his eyes were still tired, his body crying for more sleep.

He shuffled closer to Anna, breathing her in and draping an arm around her waist. She leaned into him. Ben closed his eyes and willed sleep to come back. He must have dozed for a while, but eventually his eyes opened and he had to admit defeat.

Sliding out of the bed as carefully and quietly as he could, Ben threw on some clean underwear, visited the en suite, brushed his teeth and then made his way downstairs. Humming to himself in the cold house, he put the heating on and made a cup of tea, wondering briefly if he should make Anna one just in case she woke up.

He poured the boiling water into his cup and stared out of the window as he thought. The snow had definitely stopped although everything outside was still a crisp white. How long would it take to thaw? Ben sighed and made a cup of tea for Anna, then carried both cups upstairs.

Anna was sitting up in bed, the duvet pulled up to her chin, blinking as Ben walked into the room.

'Hey. Did I wake you? I'm sorry,' Ben murmured, putting Anna's tea on the bedside table next to her.

She exhaled slowly.

'For a moment there I thought you'd gone.'

'Where would I go?' Ben asked, sliding back in beside her.

'Oh, you're freezing!' Anna flinched away from him and then took a deep breath and wrapped her naked body around his.

Ben laughed and then moaned at the joy of her heat against his chill. He kissed her hair and neck, brushing cold fingertips across her back. Anna gave a little squeal and pushed him away.

'Nope. You're too cold. And now I need to pee.'

Grinning, Ben sipped his tea while he waited for Anna to return from the bathroom. She jogged back in and slid straight under the duvet. Ben put his cup of tea down and scooped Anna into his arms.

'Now you're as cold as me,' he said, his face in her neck.

She wrapped herself about him and they stayed that way, Ben kissing her neck, until they were both warmed up. Anna slowly sat up, away from Ben, and sipped her own tea.

'Could really do with a coffee,' she murmured.

'You know it's not even seven yet?'

'What?' Anna screeched, looking around her. 'Where's my phone? How do you know it's not even seven?'

Ben showed her his own phone's screen and the time.

'Why are you awake so early?' Anna sank back into the bed, rubbing her eyes.

'I'm always awake this early.' Ben sank down

with her. They stared at one another over the top of the duvet.

'Should we go back to sleep?' Anna asked.

'Up to you,' said Ben, his hand creeping back to her. His fingers brushed over her soft skin and he tried to work out what body part it was. She grinned at him.

'That's my knee.'

'I knew that.'

Anna moved his hand to her stomach and Ben slowly moved it lower, waiting for Anna to stop him. Instead, her grin widened. She rolled on to her back and parted her legs, sighing wistfully.

'What does anyone do on Boxing Day before seven in the morning?'

Ben moved until he was pressed against her.

'I have some ideas.' He dipped beneath the duvet and in the hot darkness found her breasts.

'Best Christmas ever,' came Anna's muffled, wistful voice.

Ben agreed, although he didn't know if Anna heard him, not that it mattered.

At nine o'clock, Ben brought them toast to eat in bed, vowing to change the sheets later that day.

'Because of all the sex?' Anna asked, taking a big bite of the buttery toast.

'No, because of all the crumbs,' said Ben.

'Fair enough. I guess you might as well wait until I've gone before you change the bed because of all the sex.'

Ben didn't respond. He ate his toast and became lost in thoughts of how to keep Anna there. Banishing the thoughts as quickly as they came, he gave a sigh and finished the small breakfast. He couldn't conspire to keep her there. If she wanted to leave, then she would leave.

'Do you want to check the road later?' he managed, putting his crumb-filled plate on his bedside table.

'I guess.'

Her tone made Ben glance over. She brushed her fingers clean over her plate and placed it on her own bedside table, lying back and meeting his gaze.

'How many condoms do we have left?'

A smile picked at the corners of Ben's mouth.

'A few.'

Anna closed her eyes.

'Should I leave you with one or two? For the next damsel in distress.'

When Ben didn't laugh, she opened her eyes and looked at him. 'That was a joke.'

'I know. I just don't want you thinking that's what this was.'

'Of course I know that's not what this was! Come here.' Anna shifted over to him and placed her head on his chest, snuggling up. He wrapped his arms around her. 'I hate to be the one to tell you this, but you're covered in crumbs,' came her muffled voice.

Ben laughed and Anna sat up, brushing him

down gently.

'You'll be finding crumbs for weeks,' she told him.

'No. Because I'll change the bed,' he reminded her, pushing her long hair from her neck and chest. She moved until his hand cupped her breast and then, grinning, she leaned in to kiss him.

By the time they decided to get up, there was one condom left.

'I should probably have a quick shower,' said Anna, searching for her clothes on Ben's floor.

'I think we probably both need a shower after all that.' Ben eyed Anna as she fumbled her bra. 'We could have one together?'

Anna immediately turned back to Ben and then, after a moment's pause, threw her bra at him.

Laughing, they made their way to the en suite and showered together, taking it in turns under the hot water and cleaning one another. They rushed drying themselves and fell back onto Ben's bed to use that last condom.

'Well, that negated the whole shower, I think,' said Anna, dressing herself as Ben lay naked on his back, smiling up at the ceiling.

'Worth it,' he murmured.

Anna laughed and threw him his t-shirt. He pulled it over his head and went searching for his underwear.

'What time is it?' Anna asked, patting down her pockets.

'Eleven,' said Ben, checking his phone. 'Should we check the road? I don't want your car getting hit if people are able to drive past it. We should probably try moving it out of the way.'

'I think it broke down far enough over to the side, but that's probably a good idea.'

'The road's narrow,' said Ben, finding the rest of his clothes. 'I don't know how that tractor got past it.'

Anna looked up, eyes wide.

'Do you think my car got hit?'

'Probably not.' Ben winced. He should have thought of it earlier, but moving the broken car through thick snow would have been impossible. It could still be impossible, but if the road was clear enough, perhaps he could shovel a path to his driveway and they could push the car onto it.

He glanced at Anna's arms as she left the bedroom to look out of the hallway window. Maybe he could push and she could steer.

They pulled on coats and boots and made their way out into the still, white morning.

'Oh, this is gorgeous,' said Anna. 'All this snow and my face isn't getting wet.' She held up a hand to Ben as he went to speak. 'No snowballs this time. We don't have any protection left.'

Chuckling, Ben led Anna down the driveway to the road.

The tractor had done a good job, piling the snow on either side of the road and clearing a way through. Tyre tracks showed that some cars had already made the journey past the Old Vicarage. Anna's car, however, had taken the brunt and was now under more snow than the clouds could have possibly put on it.

'I'll get a couple of shovels,' said Ben.

When he returned, Anna was trying to dig her tyres out with her gloved hands. He passed her a shovel and they worked in silence, digging the car out and clearing the way in front.

'Now what?' Anna breathed, leaning on the shovel. 'I think I'm done.'

Ben, breathing hard, looked back to his driveway. 'I'll clear the route up there, then take the handbrake off and we'll push it onto my driveway.'

'Let me just try the engine one more time,' said Anna.

Ben didn't say anything, although he was pretty sure the whole thing would be frozen by now. The car stuttered as Ben cleared the route, and when he turned back, Anna climbed out of the car and gave a big shrug.

'Handbrake is off. Now what?'

'You steer and I'll push,' said Ben, dropping his shovel and moving behind the car.

It took a while to get the car moving, with some shouting between the two, but eventually they rocked it into motion and Anna steered it onto Ben's driveway as Ben pushed.

'That's it. Handbrake on now!' Ben shouted as

his feet touched the end of his driveway.

Anna did as he said and the car stopped and stayed put. Ben brushed the snow from his gloved hands. 'That'll do. Right, inside. Let's get a fire on and the kettle on and something to eat.'

'Oh, there's bacon, isn't there. Bacon rolls?'

Ben looked at Anna and smiled.

'I don't think I could want you more right now.'

She laughed and raced him back to the house. Given that she hadn't been pushing the car, she won the race easily. Ben shook off the snow and removed his coat and boots, as Anna did the same. At least she wasn't talking of making calls. Maybe she would want to stay after all.

25

Anna

After lunch and more coffee, Anna and Ben collapsed on the sofa and stared at the empty fireplace.

'I thought you were going to light the fire,' said Anna.

'I was, but it needs cleaning first and you need energy to clean it.' Ben sighed. 'I usually clean it first thing, but...'

'You were too busy cleaning me.' Anna giggled, turning her head to look at him beside her. Ben met her eyes and she wondered if he was thinking about his soapy hands on her body, as she was. Or the sight of his broad frame pushing her car through the snow. She looked away quickly. There could be no more sex. Not unless they could pop out to a shop, and her broken down car had just blocked Ben's driveway. She was about to point this out when Ben spoke first.

'There are things we don't need condoms for,' he said slowly.

When Anna turned back to him, he was staring at the empty fireplace again. She followed his gaze.

'This isn't about fire making, is it?'

Ben laughed and took her hand. 'Normally I wouldn't have the energy for this much exercise, even if it is sex. But...'

Anna shook her head.

'That's just the first throes of lust,' she explained. 'Give us a week and we'll calm down. Hell, give me a working car and I bet we'd slow down.'

When Ben didn't respond, she slowly turned back to him.

'I doubt it,' he murmured.

'Me too.' She leaned over and kissed him.

The afternoon proved to be a lazy one. They barely moved from the sofa, other than to put the heating on and make each other cups of tea that would go cold as their hands explored beneath clothes and they kissed each other until their lips were swollen.

How was Anna ever going to leave this? It had occurred to her that she should call someone. The breakdown service, or Mr Cuthbert who had the cottage keys. She could have asked Ben to give her a lift there. At the very least, she should find her phone. But she couldn't tear herself from Ben. If this was her life now, just the two of them in this beautiful house, making love in front of the fire every evening, then she would eventually die a happy woman.

Ben's phone beeped and they both lifted from the sofa at the sudden noise.

'Is everything okay?' Anna asked, wondering if she should take this opportunity to run upstairs and grab her own phone. She didn't move.

'Yeah.' A grin spread on Ben's face as he read the message he'd been sent. 'A friend at work's baby was due over Christmas. Look.'

He showed her the photo he'd been sent of a wrinkly newborn wrapped in a blanket covered in cartoon reindeers.

'Cute!'

'It's a girl,' said Ben.

His tone made Anna look up into his eyes.

'I told them they should name the baby after me, and guess what.'

Anna laughed.

'They've called her Ben?'

Ben shook his head and waved the phone at her until she took it and read the message.

Merry Christmas! Double presents next year because our baby arrived yesterday. She's a girl and she's perfect. Cara's doing well too. As promised, we've named our daughter after you. This is Mable Benjamina. Hope you're having a good one too.

'Benjamina!' Anna cried. 'That's so sweet. You must be so proud.' She gave Ben a sideways look. 'Do they live in London?'

Ben nodded.

'I used to stay with them sometimes when I went into the office for work, but the spare room is now the nursery.'

Anna handed Ben his phone and they both looked down at the photo of the baby.

'They must really think a lot of you to name their daughter after you,' Anna murmured.

'I think Cara just likes the name,' said Ben, putting the phone down and studying Anna. She sat back, waiting for him to finish scrutinising her, wondering if he was thinking what she was thinking.

'I should clean the fireplace,' Ben continued, kissing her wrist. 'I can light a fire and we can take these clothes off.'

Smiling, Anna leaned her head back and gave a soft laugh.

'Not yet. Dinner first. And let's not get carried away. It's been a while since I screwed up.'

'What does that mean?' Ben asked, running his hand over her clothed waist, down to her hip.

'It means that we don't have any protection left and if we do anything slightly wrong, I'll probably know about it in a couple of weeks, given my luck. That's what I mean.' Anna gave him a look and Ben hesitated, thinking this through. Anna wasn't sure if she loved or was concerned about the smile twitching at his lips.

'I'd know about it too, right?' he asked.

'Definitely.' Anna smiled and kissed his cheek. 'I know where you live,' she whispered.

Ben laughed and pulled her close, holding her tight. She hugged him back.

'I don't think that would be such a bad thing,' he whispered.

She pulled away and searched his eyes, exhaling in relief as he clarified, 'Not now. But one day?'

Anna looked around the living room, cold without the fire lit and with the snow piled up against the window, but still cosy with the Christmas tree lit up, the lights reflecting on the tinsel. The memory of the fantasy she'd made up of their child and dog in the kitchen cooking with her flashed through her mind. She saw the young child sitting by the fire, the teenager splayed out on the armchair, the toddler playing on the carpet.

'One day,' Anna agreed, 'it could be a very good thing.' She looked back to Ben. 'We can't stay like this, though, can we.'

Ben's expression fell.

'We're going to run out of food, apart from anything else,' said Anna. 'And the rest of the world is out there. I need to call people, don't I.' She stretched and sat up, immediately regretting it as Ben's hands fell away from her. 'But not yet,' she said. 'I'm hungry. How about you? Let's make some food and then I'll figure it out. Maybe I could go tomorrow instead of today.'

Ben nodded.

'Whatever you want.'

Anna stopped him as he went to stand.

'What do you want?' she asked.

Ben laughed, looking her in the eye.

'You,' he said. 'Is that not obvious?' He kissed her and then stood, leaving the room and returning with the tools to clean the fireplace. Anna watched him, wondering what her next move should be. Her phone was still on her bed. It had been over twenty-four hours since she'd last looked at it. That had to be a record. She wasn't sure she wanted to find it.

'I want you too,' she said quietly, standing and leaving the room before Ben could reply. She went into the kitchen instead of up the stairs and checked what food they had left.

'What do you normally have for Boxing Day dinner? Or is that a stupid question?' she called out.

'There are no stupid questions,' Ben shouted back. 'Sandwiches, of course.'

Anna grinned.

'A little buffet, I can do that,' she told the room, pulling the Christmas dinner leftovers from the fridge and turning on the oven. She arranged mini sausage rolls on a baking tray and placed them in the oven along with a couple of frozen bread rolls. Then she arranged the leftover turkey on a plate and found the cranberry sauce. A packet of crisps was emptied into a bowl and, as an afterthought, she chopped up some cucumber and threw some lettuce leaves and baby tomatoes into a salad bowl she found in a cupboard.

'Green stuff?' said Ben, approaching from behind and kissing her cheek, his hand on her waist.

'It may be Christmas, but we should at least pretend to have something healthy,' said Anna. 'That's why I brought the salad stuff. It'll go off otherwise.'

'Okay, but I'm not promising I'll eat any of it.' Ben disappeared through the back door, sending a rush of chilled air through the room. When he returned with wood for the fire, Anna had a silly smile on her face, pouring out two glasses of wine.

Ben went into the living room and Anna's smile fell. Her hand went to her stomach as her mind swirled. Closing her eyes, Anna steadied herself against the wave of dizziness. Leaving the wine behind, Anna wandered into the living room.

'Are you all right?' she asked.

'Yeah. Why? Are you?' Ben, crouched at the fireplace, looked at her over his shoulder.

'Yeah. I think so. Just... A strange feeling that something was about to go wrong.' She gave a short laugh. 'I guess maybe it's a good thing I'm getting premonitions now. I wonder what it could be.'

'Maybe you're hungry? Or it's lack of sleep?' Ben suggested, straightening and studying her. 'You don't feel well?'

'No, I feel fine now.' Which was true. The dizziness was gone, her vision was clear, her stomach still, as if nothing had happened. Frowning, Anna checked the time. 'No idea. I'm fine, though. Ten minutes for dinner. I'm just going to find my phone, I think it's on my bed.'

'All right.'

Anna hurried toward the stairs, remembering stories she'd heard of people having bad feelings before discovering something awful had happened to a family member. Was her father all right? Her mother?

Halfway up the stairs, there was a knock on the front door and Anna froze.

'Huh. I guess the roads really are clear,' came Ben's voice below.

In a panic, Anna rushed to the landing and grabbed her phone off the bed, in case she needed to call the police. She was back on the landing in time to watch Ben open the door, and she glanced down at her phone screen and the notifications waiting for her.

'Oh no.'

The front door opened and Anna's mother's voice rang out loudly.

'Anna! Are you here? You're the man who owns this place? Where's my daughter? Anna!'

Anna walked slowly down the stairs as Ben let her mother inside. Not just her mother. Her stepfather and their two children followed behind her.

Her mother brightened when she saw Anna.

'There you are! Come on, we're taking you home.'

'What?' Anna murmured, glancing at Ben. She'd expected a wide-eyed expression of confusion, but instead Ben seemed resigned. He hung back, eyes down after glancing fleetingly at Anna.

'No, Mum. You didn't have to come. I'm fine.' She wanted to scream and shout and throw a tantrum. She was more than fine. She was falling in love, and her mother and her stupid family had come along to ruin it.

'Thank you for looking after her,' said Anna's stepfather to Ben. 'We'll take her off your hands now.'

Anna's features darkened.

'Take me off... I...' She opened and closed her mouth, the sudden rage blocking all comprehensive thoughts.

Ben shook his head.

'It really has been no trouble,' he told them quietly.

'I'm hungry!' stated one of the children.

Anna clenched her eyes shut.

'How did you get here so fast?' She rubbed her forehead, trying to ease the headache that was already building.

'The four-by-four. Of course. As soon as we heard the snow had stopped,' her mother explained, stopping one of the children from following his nose to the kitchen.

'Worth every penny, that car.' Her stepfather grinned at her. 'Something does smell good.'

'No!' Anna shouted.

Everyone stopped. 'That smell is dinner for me and Ben, you're not having any of it.'

'Don't be ridiculous, the children are hungry,' said her mother.

'This isn't your house.' Anna's teeth were gritted. She finished walking down the stairs, positioning herself next to Ben and between her family and the kitchen. She couldn't have stopped them turning up at Ben's door but she could stop them ransacking his kitchen.

'There's salad,' came Ben's mutter in her ear.

Heart pounding, Anna caught her smile before it could grow. She met his eyes for one blissful moment.

'There's salad, if you want that.' She turned back to the children, who both pulled faces.

'Salad doesn't smell like that,' her stepfather grumbled.

'I know,' said her mother. 'That cottage is still yours, right? Let's go there and have something to eat. Spend the night. It's too late to go home now anyway. Yes? Right. Everyone back in the car. Anna, go get your things.'

The floor fell away from Anna's feet.

26

Ben

'I'm hungry now!' screamed one of the children.

Ben flinched against the noise and was acutely aware of Anna tensing beside him. There hadn't been this many people in his house in such a long time, Ben wasn't sure what to do with himself. Frozen against the wall, aware of Anna's stepfather to his left, he kept his eyes down, his mind empty of ways out of this.

'I'm not going, Mum,' came Anna's calm voice.

'Of course you are. We didn't come all this way to rescue you only for you to not come with us. Now, go get your things. And could we possibly use your toilet?' she asked Ben, making a show of almost crossing her legs.

Forcing himself to breathe, Ben nodded and pointed to the cupboard under the stairs where the downstairs toilet was hidden.

'Just in there,' he murmured.

'Thank you. Steve, get everyone back in the car. Anna, when I'm out, you'll have your stuff and then we're leaving.'

She vanished into the cupboard, leaving Steve and the two children, who must have been around five and eight – although Ben wasn't great with ageing children – staring hungrily at him. If this was a horror movie, they'd be about to eat him, he thought.

'I'm still hungry!' shouted the maybe eight-year-old boy.

Anna turned in a flounce and stomped into the kitchen. She came back with some slices of the cucumber.

'That's all there is.' She handed them to the boy, who stared at her proffered hand and then raised his chin defiantly.

He's about to scream, Ben realised, half-closing his eyes in anticipation.

'Oh, come on, Anna,' said Steve. The man turned to Ben. 'You don't have anything proper? They're children.'

'Who you should have brought food for,' Anna stated. 'They're your responsibility. You put them in that monster car of yours and drove them all this way – for no reason, I might add – and now you're expecting Ben to feed them? No. Go back to the car and wait for Mum.' Anna crossed her arms and stared Steve down.

She was a braver person than Ben.

He watched, waiting to see what her stepfather would do.

Steve took a step forward, closer to Anna, ignoring Ben, and hissed in her face, 'It's Christmas, Anna. You've upset your mother enough.'

Ben took in a deep breath, his hands curling into fists at his sides as Anna flinched.

'It's okay,' said Ben softly. 'I'll get the kids something to eat.'

He turned away to the kitchen, happy to be away from the heat in the hallway. He heard no voices while he was gone and assumed Anna and Steve were just staring at each other, until one of the children evidently punched the other and they started screaming at one another. Steve's voice rose above the cacophony and Ben grabbed the biscuit tin.

'Here,' he said, offering the open tin to the bickering children. 'Help yourselves.'

Anna made a noise, but before she could form words, both children had quietened and shoved their hands into the tin, each pulling out three or four biscuits.

'Oh, erm...'

'One each,' Anna demanded.

'No, it's okay. If it's okay with...' Ben looked up at Steve, who shrugged, disinterested. Ben put the lid on the tin and backed away.

A flushing toilet sounded and the downstairs cupboard door opened to reveal Anna's mother, stepping into the hallway, brushing down her dress. She stopped when she saw her family hadn't moved.

'What did I say?' she almost shouted. 'Car. Now. All of you. Where did you get those biscuits?'

'The man who kidnapped Anna gave them to us,' said the boy.

'I didn't—'

'He didn't kidnap me,' said Anna, interrupting Ben's quiet voice as his stomach dropped to his knees. 'Is that what you've been telling them?'

'Oh, children make up things.' Her mother brushed the words from the air.

'And they repeat what adults tell them,' said Anna. There was a new quiver in her voice and Ben snapped up to look at her. He edged closer.

'Are you all right?' he whispered.

'I'm so sorry about all this,' she whispered back as her mother herded Steve and the children out of the house. 'I should have kept my phone on me.' She showed him the latest messages from her mother.

According to the weather app the snow has stopped? So we'll come get you.

Anna? We're going to come get you. Not today because it's Christmas. We'll come tomorrow.

Anna?? Are you there? Where are you? We're coming to get you. Be with you in a few hours.

Anna!?! Hello?! We're nearly there. Which house is it?

Anna!!! We've found your car. Coming in.

There were two missed calls.

Ben stared at the messages.

'I'm sorry,' he murmured.

'Why are you sorry? I'm the one who left my phone on my bed and didn't think to check it. Like an idiot. And now they just barge into your home and steal all your biscuits.' Anna sighed. 'Maybe I should go with them. You'd be better off without me.'

Ben's brain started a warning siren, panic flooding through him.

'No, no, I wouldn't. It's okay. I don't mind. They're only biscuits. And the kids were hungry.'

'They always do this,' Anna muttered, not hearing him. 'They're so blinkered. They just rush in and don't even think about what their kids might need. I mean, I bet they did bring food but they probably ate it all in the car. And they know they do that, so why didn't they bring more? Why couldn't the kids stay in the car? Why did all of them have to come to the front door?'

Ben opened his mouth, desperate to ask Anna to stay, but her mother got there first.

'Oh, you were right about Brad.'

As one, Anna and Ben turned to her.

'Why do you say that?' Anna asked slowly, her eyes narrowing.

'He turned up at the house on Christmas Eve. In the evening!' She shook her head in disgust. 'Of all the times. I'd just gotten the kids down. You know how excited they get. He woke them up. Took us another hour to get them back to sleep.'

'Why did he show up at yours?'

'Going on and on about how he couldn't get through to you and could we phone you for him.'

Anna exhaled in a growl.

'That's because I've blocked him on everything.'

'Well, you were right, he is a pain.'

'A pain?' Anna screeched. 'He cheated on me, Mum! Calling him a pain hardly covers it. He's a—'

'Anna! Anyway, Steve sent him on his way.' Her mother turned to Ben, as if seeing him for the first time, looking him up and down. 'Thank you so much for taking care of my little girl. I can see now that she was being well looked after.'

Anna, mouth open, stared at her mother, turned to Ben and then whipped back to her mother.

'I—Little? Well...'

'Actually, I'm sort of glad it all happened,' Ben said quietly, his eyes back on the floor. The carpet was getting so threadbare. How had he not noticed it before? 'This is the best Christmas I've had in a long time.' Or at least, it had been the best Christmas. Until now. He swallowed hard, glancing up to find Anna smiling softly at him.

'Hmm. Well, thank you again. Come on, Anna. What shall we do with your car?'

'It won't start, Mum. How about you guys get back home and I'll stay here until I can get it fixed?'

'Oh, no. That's asking far too much of, erm...'

'Ben,' murmured Ben.

'Yes, Ben. I'm Marie, thank you again for your hospitality towards my daughter. And anyway, we have our plan. We're going to your cottage. The photos looked nice enough. Do you have the keys?'

'No. I have to call someone to get them, and—'

'Well, give them a call then.'

'But—'

'Anna, we have driven a long way to come and get you. On Boxing Day. You didn't answer any of my calls or messages. For all I knew you were dead inside this man's freezer – no offence.'

Ben shook his head.

'None taken,' he whispered to the floor.

'So give this key person a call and let's get going.'

Anna blinked and pursed her lips.

'I don't have any food, Mum. Me and Ben ate it all.'

Her mother shrugged.

'Oh, that's all right. There's a shop in the village, isn't there? I think they're open. We'll check in there, and if not, we'll find something. It'll be fine. Come on. Go get your stuff. Do you have any stuff?' Marie looked about her and then gave her daughter's clothes an appraising look.

Anna sighed.

'Oh for crying out loud, Anna. Who's the person with the keys?'

'Mr Cuthbert, but—'

'Give me his number.'

'Mum—'

'Anna!'

Anna flinched and then unlocked her phone, searching for the right number.

'Here,' she muttered, passing it to her mother.

'Thank you.' Marie hit the call button and then vanished from the house, disappearing out into the driveway and closing the front door behind her after shouting over her shoulder, 'Go get your bags!'

Anna and Ben watched her go.

'We could lock the door,' Anna whispered.

Ben, his stomach twisted in knots, shook his head.

'I'll do whatever you want,' he told her gently, 'but they're your family. And it's Christmas. Maybe you should...'

Anna's eyes widened as she looked up at him.

'You want me to go with them?'

That was the last thing Ben wanted. His frown was so deep this time that it gave him an immediate headache, the creases digging into his skull. When he didn't answer, Anna huffed and turned her back on him, heading to the stairs.

'Fine. I'll go.'

'Anna, wait.'

Ben followed her, jogging up the stairs to catch up. He followed her into her bedroom and watched as she threw clothes into her bag. It didn't take long.

'I didn't mean that.'

He followed her into the bathroom where she gathered her toothbrush, pushing past him to throw it in her bag.

'Then what did you mean?' she asked, turning to face him on the landing, bag in hand.

'I... I just...'

Anna sighed and looked past him.

'I just want to do the right thing,' he murmured.

'Well, I don't,' Anna told him. 'I want you to tell me what you want. Whether it's the right thing or not. Should I strip the bed?'

Flummoxed, Ben looked over his shoulder to the bed.

'Erm...'

'Ben, do you want me?'

'Anna!'

Marie's voice filled the house. Ben couldn't breathe. Anna raised an eyebrow at him and then nodded, her lips pressed tightly together, her chin quivering in such a way that it made Ben's chest tighten.

'Well, there you go.' She walked down the stairs and Ben watched her go with horror.

'No, wait.' He rushed after her. 'I just...'

'Thank you for a magical Christmas,' Anna told him once she'd reached the front door. She went up on tiptoe and kissed the corner of his mouth. Their eyes met for one tantalising moment. 'I'll be back later for my car,' she murmured, turning away.

Ben watched her get into the giant four-by-four driven by Steve, and stood stunned as the car pulled out and drove away.

The silence that followed, along with the smell of burning sausage rolls, was unbearable.

27

Anna

Anna needed to be sick. Nausea swelled and swirled around her stomach, bile dancing up her throat, but she swallowed hard, pushing it all down. The four-by-four pushing over the snow in bumps and slides didn't help, neither did her half-siblings arguing over who knew what beside her on the back seats.

She stared out the window, watching the hedges and sporadic large houses of the country road pass by, until they reached the end of the lane and moved out onto a main road into the village.

Marie and Steve were chatting in the front, but not to Anna. She was stuck in the back, with the children, being ignored, as she was every Christmas. Gritting her teeth, Anna considered opening the door and flinging herself out. Steve picked up speed and soon it was too late to consider that idea.

'I bet it feels good to be out of that house, huh, Anna?' came her mother's voice.

Anna tried to smile and nod, but instead she barely reacted.

'He seemed like a nice boy, though. You were very lucky.'

Anna nodded. She had been lucky.

'We'll pop to the shop, before it closes, and get whatever they have, and then go get the keys. Yes?'

'I want chips!' shouted the five-year-old beside Anna.

'Takeaway!' shouted the older boy.

'Are there any good takeaways around here?' Marie asked Anna, turning round in her front seat.

Anna stared at her mother.

'I don't know,' she snapped.

'All right. Sorry. Just thought you might have done some research.'

'No, Mum. I came up here to have a Christmas on my own, and I brought all my own food. I was getting a delivery, remember? But it got cancelled because of the snow.'

Marie sighed and Anna sat back, her stomach churning.

'Yes, I'm well aware that your plan was to come up here to get away from us. But we've rescued you, Anna, and it would be nice to have some appreciation.'

'I didn't need rescuing! I told you that.'

'Of course you did. Don't be ridiculous. Oh, look, there's a chippy.' Marie pointed to the shop as Steve drove past and into the village centre. 'And a corner shop. Pull over here, I'll see what they have.'

'I don't think you can park here, Mum.'

'Can't see any yellow lines,' said Steve, grinning as he pulled the huge car over. 'Thanks to all the snow.' He gestured for Marie to hurry. 'Go with your mum,' he said to Anna as Marie got out of the car and slammed the door shut. 'Help her out.'

Growling softly to herself, Anna gladly fell out of the car and stomped through the snow, following her mother.

The warmth of the shop blasted her in the face as she stepped inside, the door shutting the cold out behind her. Anna took a moment to glance around and then spotted her mother waiting for her, holding a basket.

'Come on, then,' said Marie, wandering down an aisle. 'This is a big corner shop.'

'It's a Co-op, Mum.'

'Is it? Well, that's nice. I didn't think they had those all the way out here.'

Anna gave her mother a look but resisted rolling her eyes. She couldn't help the sigh, though. Marie gave her a sideways look.

'I'm sorry we bustled in like that,' she told her daughter gently. 'And I'm sorry I brought the kids inside. Steve got them out of their seats.'

'Hmm.'

'I'm sorry if I embarrassed you.'

Anna relented, softening a little as Marie put a couple of tins of baked beans in the basket.

'You didn't embarrass me. You just…interrupted.'

Marie looked up at Anna.

'Interrupted? What, dinner?'

'…No.'

Marie's eyes widened.

'Anna!' she whispered as loud as she dared. 'You weren't…'

'Well, not at that exact moment, no.' Anna closed her eyes, wishing she hadn't mentioned it.

'Do you know how dangerous that is? You don't know him. What if he'd chopped you up and put you in his freezer?'

'What's this obsession you have with being put in the freezer?' Anna hissed as a man with his own heavy-laden basket passed them.

'It happens, you know!' Marie hissed back. 'I've heard all about it.'

'You've been listening to those podcasts again. I told you to give those a break.'

'They're educational,' said Marie, lifting her chin and putting a load of sliced bread in the basket. Anna pulled a face.

'Is this for tonight? Are you making beans on toast for Boxing Day?'

Marie stared down at the basket.

'Nothing wrong with beans on toast.'

Anna sighed again and took the basket from her mother, emptying its contents on a nearby shelf. She marched to the next aisle and Marie trailed behind. Finding the packs of sausage rolls, pork pies and the last pigs in blankets, Anna threw a couple of packs of each into the basket and moved on.

'So, you and this…'

'Ben.'

'Ben were…' Marie looked up at Anna.

'Does it matter? It doesn't matter. I was having a fun Christmas, that's all. Not the one I planned, probably much more fun. But I see why you came. And I'm sorry. I should have kept my phone on me.'

'But you were preoccupied.'

'I was.' Anna added a tub of coleslaw and a bottle of mayonnaise and another of ketchup to the basket.

'Well, you'll see him again when we get your car back, I suppose. If we can find someone to fix it. At the very least, we'll get it moved so that Ben can have his driveway back.'

'Yes, you realise we've left him blocked in at his own house. What if he runs out of food?'

'Oh, he'll be fine. We'll go back tomorrow morning and move the car.' Marie waved away Anna's concerns and Anna gritted her teeth.

'Or,' she said, returning to the bread aisle and finding the last packet of partially-baked baguettes, 'you drop me back at Ben's and then you, Steve and the kids go spend the night at the cottage.'

'What? Without you?'

'Without me. I can move my car, apologise to

Ben, and then you can pick me up in the morning and drag me back to my rubbish life.'

Anna froze when she realised what she'd said. Marie had stopped, staring at her daughter.

'Why is your life rubbish?'

'It doesn't matter, Mum. Come on, let's get this to the till.'

'No, hang on.' Marie grabbed her daughter's arm, stopping Anna with a jolt. 'What do you mean? You've got people who love you, a roof over your head and a good job. And you have what looks to me like maybe two men interested in you. What does this Ben do, anyway? Is it better than Brad's job?'

Anna met her mother's eyes and tried to stop what felt like steam from exploding through her ears.

'Ben's a financial advisor—'

'—Oh dear—'

'—in London, and he owns that house. The Old Vicarage. And...what do you mean, "oh dear"?'

'Come on, he works in finance. He's one of those.'

Anna gawped at her mother.

'He's the nicest, loveliest—'

'You're probably better off without him.'

'Oh, yes, because who on earth would want to be with a gorgeous, kind man with a good job and a beautiful house?' Anna shouted. She pressed her lips together, heat rushing up to her cheeks. Staring down at the floor, the women waited in silence to see if anyone had heard. Of course they had heard, Anna had been loud, but no one said anything.

'So why is your life rubbish?' Marie asked calmly, taking the basket from Anna and heading towards the tills. Anna watched her mother's back.

'Because I lost my job,' she said quietly, partly hoping her mother wouldn't hear.

Marie stopped so suddenly she almost tripped over her own foot. Anna grimaced as her mother turned on her heel and marched back to her.

'Excuse me?'

Taking a deep breath, Anna repeated herself. 'I lost my job.'

'You were fired?'

'Made redundant.' Anna shook her head.

Marie blinked, staring through her daughter.

'What about your rent?'

'I have savings, Mum.'

'And you're job hunting?'

'Yes.'

'Have you had any interviews?'

'Not yet.'

Marie met her daughter's eyes and sighed.

'Do you need help?'

Anna gave a small smile.

'No, I'm all right. Thank you.'

'Don't let that situation lead you into thinking you need to hook up with a wealthy man.' Marie turned back and headed towards the tills at the front of the shop. Anna followed.

'It's not like that,' she said quietly once she reached her mother. 'Ben and I... There was something real there.' She stopped, realising just how much that was true, like a light going on in her head and filtering down through her body.

'No, I'm not having this. It's Christmas,' said Marie, approaching the cashier and putting down her basket. 'You're coming to the cottage. We'll stop over to move your car in the morning and then you're coming home with us. You can move in with us until you find a new job.' Marie nodded and turned her full attention to the cashier, pulling out her purse to pay for everything.

Anna stared at her, bewildered.

'But I don't want to,' she said quietly.

'Nonsense. It'll do you good.'

The cashier put everything into a bag, and they left, heading back outside to the snowy darkness. Anna stood by the car, staring at the door, wondering if she could just turn and run away, how far she'd get.

'Anna! Get in.'

Sighing, holding back tears, Anna got into the car, beside her half-siblings who were complaining about being hungry and bored. Steve pulled the car back onto the road and Marie gave him directions to Mr Cuthbert's, where they'd pick up the cottage keys.

Anna barely heard any of it.

Her mind was in a spiral, searching for a way out of this. Even if she could find a way out of the car, through the snow, back to Ben, what would she do after Christmas? She'd have to face the real world again eventually. Her mother was right. Who knew how long it would take for her to find another job, and there was her rent and bills to pay and food to buy. Anna bit on her lip in an attempt to hold back the tears.

She needed help and there didn't seem another option. Perhaps her father would offer her a room, but he didn't have the space and there wasn't much difference between his home with his family or her mother's with her family.

I don't fit anywhere, Anna thought, looking up and out of the window to the silent snow-covered fields, shining in the moonlight.

Mr Cuthbert lived in a beautiful, small period cottage with such a large garden that it made Anna's head spin. She plastered on a grin and greeted him, thanking him for his help when she'd first become stranded at Ben's. Marie made some small talk and took the cottage keys, and then they were back in the car. Anna kept Mr Cuthbert's closed front door in her sight for as long as possible.

The cottage Anna had booked was picturesque, especially in the snow. A little two-bedroom affair with a thatched roof and short fence around the front garden. Steve pulled into the gravel driveway and turned off the engine.

'Everybody out.'

Anna climbed out of the car and stood staring at what was supposed to have been her ideal Christmas alone, away from the family. Behind her came the shouts and screams of her siblings, Steve telling them to shut up as Marie picked up the shopping and carried it to the cottage's wooden front door.

Snow was piled up against the door and Marie kicked at it ineffectively until Steve came along and scooped the offending snow away.

'Anna! Get the kids out, will you?' he shouted as Marie unlocked the door.

Anna froze, her legs twitching, urging her back to the road. Blinking hard, she forced herself to turn and help her siblings out of their car seats. Without a thank you or kind word, the children ran into the cottage, lights appearing at the little windows as Anna closed the car doors and leaned against the black vehicle, still hurriedly considering escape routes.

The cottage was soon filled with the sound of the children running around, choosing their bedroom. Her mother and Steve would have the other bedroom. Anna would be consigned to the sofa, but only after her mother and Steve had decided to go to bed.

Anna clenched her eyes shut and imagined she was back in the Old Vicarage, in the warmth of the cosy living room, surrounded by fairy lights.

Snuggled against Ben. Ben who was now alone. Had he taken the sausage rolls out of the oven?

'Anna? Come on! You're letting all the cold in!' came Steve's shout.

Anna shuffled her way to the front door and stood on the periphery. The cottage hallway was enticing. Steve was already in the living room, trying to light the fire, although from the bangs and swearing, it didn't sound like he was having much luck. Her mother was in the kitchen, trying to work out the oven. The children were upstairs.

It passed through Anna's mind that she'd inevitably lose her deposit.

She stepped into the cottage but didn't close the door. She couldn't bring herself to do it. On her left was a little table with a landline phone and a pretty notepad and pencil. Anna blinked at them and then, in a panic, grabbed the pencil and notepad.

Having scribbled her note, she left it on the front doormat, shut the door and ran.

> *Sorry Mum.*
> *I love you so much.*
> *I'm fine. I'm back at Ben's.*
> *Pick me up in the morning.*
> *There should instructions for the oven in the*
> *welcome pack.*
> *Merry Christmas.*
> *xxxx*

28

Ben

The sausage rolls were the nice side of burnt, meaning that they were crispy, leaving flakes of pastry all over Ben's plate. The bread was equally nice, the butter melting into it. He even ate some of the lettuce leaves, thinking about Anna the entire time.

The television played in the background, he didn't even know what was on. He ate slowly, his stomach in knots, forcing down the food and trying to not notice how unbearably quiet the house was.

Had it always been this quiet?

Anna had forgotten her Christmas decorations, the plastic tree was still in the corner festooned with fairy lights. They blinked and beat out the pattern of Ben's heart. He finished eating and sat back, hand on his belly, nausea swelling up inside.

The fire remained unlit. He just didn't have the energy or see the point in lighting it. The fireplace was clean and ready to go, but what was the point without Anna beside him?

Ben sighed, frowning to himself.

He'd never had issue with lighting the fire before Anna had arrived on his front doorstep. She couldn't have stayed, he knew that. Eventually his life would have gone back to normal, but in those sweet hours she'd been there, he'd given hope to the idea that she could have become his new normal. Which was ridiculous. He hadn't even wanted her there when she'd first arrived.

He just needed to get used to being alone again. And the silence. The never-ending silence.

Ben turned up the volume on the TV and tried to pay attention to some vets in Yorkshire helping a cow giving birth. Sighing, he switched the channel to the ending of Jumanji. Ben gave a small smile. It was a classic film, as far as he was concerned. He watched the last twenty minutes and tensed up again as the credits rolled. Sipping his wine, he waited to see what was on next. Another Indiana Jones film, the voiceover announced. Groaning, Ben got to his feet and took his plate into the kitchen. He stood by the sink, hands on the worktop, and stared out of the window. In the light reflecting from the kitchen he could make out the mess he and Anna had made in the snow on his back lawn. Where they'd thrown snowballs at each other, where they'd lain beside one another and made snow angels before ruining them. The feel of Anna's wet jumper and hot skin beneath his frozen fingers, the electricity as he'd scooped his arms around her waist.

Ben was smiling into the window but his chest ached like nothing he'd felt before. He took his bottle of wine into the living room and topped up his glass. Of course he'd felt pain like this before, he was divorced! He must have felt this pain then.

Ben sipped his wine and tried to think back, acutely remembering the agony of finding out his wife was cheating and lying to him. This was a different sort of pain. This was less crushing, more gaping. A hole opening inside him. An Anna-shaped hole.

Mentally shaking himself, Ben tried to think back to the divorce itself. The stress and worry and pain of leaving behind all that he knew. Being alone again. The pity from his friends and family.

Still, it wasn't the same pain as this.

Ben drained the last of his wine.

He couldn't live like this. It had been an hour and the emptiness was too much. If only he'd put his foot down, said what he'd meant to say, done everything he could to convince Anna of how he felt, how he wanted her to stay, how she could stay as long as she liked. Days, weeks, months. Years. Ben wanted her to stay years.

'This is stupid,' he muttered.

Without giving it much more thought, he jumped to his feet and turned off the TV. He double checked the oven was off and then grabbed his coat, pulled on his boots and grabbed his keys. He stopped as he opened the front door. Anna's car was blocking his driveway.

With a sigh, he trudged outside and tripped on something. Looking down to his feet, in the dim light from his porch, he made out the glint of something metallic in the snow. Crouching, Ben laughed out loud.

Anna had dropped her keys. Maybe when they'd moved the car, maybe when she'd left with her family. Either way, here they were.

He gripped them in his fist and rushed over to her car, unlocking it, taking a seat, pushing down the clutch, taking of the handbrake and letting the car roll backwards. He steered it as best he could to the side of the road, just outside his house. Jumping out, he locked it and ran back up his driveway to his own car, the wine inside him sloshing a little.

He stopped and thought back to how much he'd drunk. One glass and a couple of sips. Surely that would be okay.

Opening his car door, he fell inside and started the ignition. It grumbled to a start, unhappy about the cold, complaining about what the point of the garage was if he wasn't going to put the car inside when it snowed. Ben agreed and promised that next time he'd keep the car warm in the garage. But first, he had to tell Anna how he felt. She needed the chance to make a decision with all of the facts.

Nodding to himself, Ben put the car lights on, giving his driveway an eery glow, and drove onto the road. He made his way steadily over the snow to the village, trying to remember where Anna had said the cottage was.

Still clueless by the time he reached the village's high street, he stopped outside the Co-op and gave it some thought.

'Ben Wilmslow?'

The voice was muffled but loud enough to catch Ben's attention. He turned to find Maureen from the Co-op waving at him. She was bundled up against the snow but wore her uniform underneath, stepping out of the shop and wandering over. He wound his window down.

'I was hoping that was you,' she said, approaching carefully, arms out to keep her balance where the snow was turning to ice.

'I'm looking for someone,' he told her. 'And I've no idea where she is. Except she's in a cottage somewhere around here. Are you all right?'

'I'm fine, I'm fine. Lovely young woman? Long, dark hair? She came in with an older woman, similar complexion. They were with one of those horrible big cars, all black and shiny. Kids in the back.'

'That's them!' Heart thumping, Ben swivelled in his seat and looked past her to the Co-op. 'They came in?'

'Bought a load of food, arguing and chatting.' Maureen nodded. 'She said how she'd been spending time with the nice young man in the Old Vicarage – that's you – and how much she'd been enjoying it.' There was a twinkle in Maureen's eye that Ben tried to ignore.

'Did they say where they were going?'

'Getting the keys to a cottage and staying there the night, apparently,' said Maureen. 'Which is funny, because old Vic Cuthbert was in the other day saying how the poor girl who'd rented the Murray's cottage had been caught in the snow and couldn't make it. He was meant to pass the keys on, and did I know anyone who could go rescue her. Well, I didn't. And sounds like that was for the best. Hmm?'

Ben nodded.

'Absolutely. So they've gotten the keys from him?'

'Sounds like.'

'Where is he?'

With a cunning smile, Maureen leaned closer to the car.

'I can do you one better,' she said. 'I know where the Murray's cottage is.'

She gave Ben careful directions to the cottage. He thanked her, making a mental note to buy her something after all this was done, checked she was okay on the snow and then, at her insistence, drove away.

He left the village, driving down the snow-covered roads, following Maureen's directions. The snow sucked the noise from the outside world, leaving the countryside beautiful but dangerous looking. He passed a few other cars as he went, presumably families on their way home from a Christmas hurriedly spent with loved ones. Or on their way to a Boxing Day feast somewhere warm.

Ben gave a shiver and turned on the car's heater.

He found the cottage, thatched roof sticking out from a layer of snow against a backdrop of a pretty cottage garden and large, flat fields. The lights were on at the windows and smoke billowed from the chimney. Ben turned his lights and engine off and sat, watching the windows for any sign of Anna.

There was a peek of Steve, brandishing a beer, and the top of Marie's head as he passed her a drink. Flickers of colour against the wall suggested the television was on. The lights upstairs were off, but whether that meant the children were in bed, Ben didn't know.

The rush of adrenaline had been dampened by the reality of seeing Marie and Steve through the window. Swallowing hard, Ben got out of the car and walked up to the front door. He cleared his throat, took a deep breath and filled his mind with Anna, before knocking on the door.

There came the sound of a raised voice from inside and then the door opened, revealing Steve at his full height.

Ben did his best not to shrink back.

'You? What do you want?'

Ben cleared his throat again.

'I'm here to speak to Anna. She...erm...left her keys behind.'

Steve narrowed his eyes at Ben.

'Is this a joke?'

'No. Why?' Ben's stomach turned. Where was Anna?

Steve turned back inside the cottage and shouted, 'Marie!'

Ben flinched and shuffled back a little, his boots sliding on the snow. Anna's mother appeared behind Steve and peered around him. Her eyes widened when she recognised Ben and she stepped forward.

'You! Where is she? You brought her back?'

Ben blinked.

'What? Is Anna here?'

'No. She's with you.'

For the second time that day, the ground fell away from Ben.

'She's not with me,' he breathed.

'She left this note.' Marie turned away and reappeared, passing a slip of paper to Ben. It was written in pencil and Ben had to step closer to the light of the cottage to read it, which he did three times. He scoured his memory, had he passed someone walking through the snow on his way there?

'Did she take a car?' he asked weakly, turning to stare at Steve's four-by-four.

'What car would she take?' Steve muttered. 'Is she isn't with you and she isn't here, then where is she?'

Ben had some ideas.

'This is all your fault,' Marie shouted.

Ben stepped back again, his hand squeezing so tightly around his keys that they dug painfully into his flesh.

'We have to find her,' she said to Steve, gripping on to him. 'Go find her.'

Ben turned back to his car.

'I know where she is,' he told them. 'I'll find her and ask her to call you.'

'I'll come too,' said Steve, reaching for his shoes.

'No, it's all right. I'll take my car,' said Ben, rushing away and shouting behind him. 'I'll get her to call you!'

'You'll bring her back here!' Marie screeched before pushing Steve. 'Go with him. Or go in your car.'

Steve met Ben's eyes for a moment and shrugged.

'He'll be fine. You have half an hour!' he yelled at Ben. 'Then I'm coming after you.'

Steve shut the door, although Ben could still hear Marie yelling. With a shudder, he went back to his own car and plonked into the driver's seat, trying to think like Anna. At the cottage window, two small faces peered out at him. One waved.

He waved back, started the ignition and, with a shudder, reversed away from the cottage and back onto the road.

29
Anna

'Such a dangerous thing to do. You could have died. Imagine that. Would have broken my heart.'

Anna stared out of the car window as they drove through the village, past the Co-op.

'I know. It was stupid. But I didn't know what else to do. I could have stolen Steve's keys, I guess, then stolen his car. But that would have stranded them. And they have the little ones.'

Mr Cuthbert shook his head as he turned down the road that led out of the village.

'Anything could have happened,' he murmured.

'I know. That's why I called you,' Anna explained-ed. 'I really am grateful for the help.'

'Oh, don't you worry,' said Mr Cuthbert. 'Truth be told, lovely Maureen, who works at the Co-op, she overheard you and your mum chatting when you were in buying food.'

'Oh?'

'And she called me once you'd left. Told me how there was a lovely young lady in the shop talking as if she were in love with Ben Wilmslow of the Old Vicarage. I've never met the man, myself, but Maureen sees him in the shop quite a bit. We all knew his uncle. Lovely man. Had only kind words for everyone and lots of them about his little nephew.'

Anna smiled, a warmth spreading through her chest at the thought of Ben being talked about by his uncle in such a way.

'And she mentioned how this young lady was arguing with who Maureen assumed was her mother about not being able to stay with poor Ben. That they were going to the cottage and did I suppose that was the Murray's cottage. Well, I filled her in and I apologise for that. None of our business, I know.'

'It's okay,' Anna said quietly. 'I don't mind.'

'So of course I was glad when you called. That lad deserves some happiness. I'm not sure what he's been through, but Maureen says he's always frowning. Have you noticed that?'

Anna laughed and nodded.

'Sure have.'

'I know his uncle doted on him. Losing him must have hurt. It's hard to go through something like that.' He gave Anna a sideways glance, perhaps hoping for more information, but Anna wasn't about to give any. She only nodded, agreeing wholeheartedly.

'Here we are, then.'

Mr Cuthbert slowed down, although he was already crawling along in the snow.

Anna's heart sank when she saw the Old Vicarage in darkness, and then her stomach twisted at the sight of her car back on the road.

'He's not here,' she murmured.

'Well, go check, just in case,' said Mr Cuthbert, pulling his car over so it faced Anna's. She threw herself out and rushed up the driveway. Ben's car was gone, but she knocked on the door anyway.

Hopping from foot to foot, Anna waited. The silence was deafening. Ben wasn't home. How long ago had he left? Where had he gone? Perhaps to the shop, or maybe he'd packed a bag and headed to London to get away from everything that had happened.

A hand on her stomach to ease the nausea, Anna turned back to Mr Cuthbert's car. She gave her own car a fleeting look. She could try moving it back onto Ben's drive, so it was out of the way, but decided that Mr Cuthbert had done her enough favours for a few years, at least.

'Where now?' he asked when she climbed back into his little car.

Anna sighed.

'I don't know. Where would he go? If he's gone to

London, I can't follow him. If he's gone to the shop, then maybe he'll be back soon?' She glanced up at the dark house. 'Back to the cottage, then. I guess.'

Mr Cuthbert turned the car around and headed back to the village. They drove in silence, Anna staring ahead, lost in her own thoughts of what she would do next. What choice did she have? She'd go back to the cottage, get lectured by her mother, wait for them to go to bed so she could pretend to sleep on the sofa, and in the morning they'd drive home. She'd move in with them, most likely end up looking after the children every day while she searched for a job that it felt like she'd never find.

Ben would be lost to her.

Her vision blurred as tears filled her eyes and tumbled down her cheeks. She sniffed as quietly as possible, not wanting Mr Cuthbert to know she was crying.

'Huh,' said Mr Cuthbert as they reached the village high street. The road was lit up with Christmas lights and streetlights, along with some windows in the flats above the dark shops, and the bright blue from the Co-op's sign. The shop's internal lights switched off as they approached and a woman stepped out to lock the doors.

'Is that Maureen?' Anna asked, trying to keep her voice steady.

'It is. I might stop and see if she wants a lift. Do you mind?'

'Of course not.'

Mr Cuthbert slowed and pulled to a stop outside the shop.

'Maureen!'

'Vic! Fancy seeing you here.' Maureen's eyes flicked to Anna and she smiled. 'Hello, again.'

'Hi.' Anna attempted a smile and Maureen's face twitched as she noticed Anna had been crying.

'What's going on here, then?'

'Looking for that Ben lad,' said Mr Cuthbert. 'But he wasn't home. Would you like a lift?'

Maureen wrapped her coat about her and nodded.

'Oh, yes, please. If you don't mind.'

'Of course not.'

'Here, take my seat. I'll go in the back,' said Anna, opening her door and stepping out. She'd just opened the back door, ready to climb in, when a car driving past them stopped with a loud crunch. The driver's door opened and Anna watched, dumbfounded, as Ben stepped out and stared at her.

Grinning, new tears in her eyes, Anna tripped over Mr Cuthbert's car as she went to rush around it to Ben. He matched her pace, moving forwards, his arms out to catch her.

'I didn't know where you'd gone,' she said.

'Your mum said you'd left,' he said at the same time.

They grinned at one another. Anna wiped her cheeks with her cold, bare hands and, frowning with concern, Ben pulled her in close. She hugged him tight.

'I thought you'd gone to London and left and I'd never see you again,' she said into his coat.

Ben chuckled against her hair.

'I went to find you,' he murmured into her ear. 'I had to find you.'

Anna pulled away a little.

'You did? Why?'

Ben brushed at her wet cheek with his thumb, smiling down at her.

'Because I had to tell you…everything. How amazing you made this Christmas. How you fill my house and life with light and warmth. How easy you make everything. How quiet everything is without you there. And cold. How much I missed you the moment you left. How I never wanted you to leave in the first place.'

'I never wanted to leave either,' Anna murmured, her body tingling, the cold forgotten as she looked up and saw only Ben. She stopped herself from saying more.

'You left the cottage to come find me?' Ben asked, taking her hands in his and enveloping them in warmth.

She nodded.

'Walked through the snow, she did! Like an idiot! Could have died!' shouted Mr Cuthbert from the pavement. Maureen shushed him and elbowed him gently.

Ben and Anna turned back to one another.

'You walked through the snow to get back to me? With your luck?' said Ben, grinning.

'Yeah. I sort of, you know, thought – hoped – you were worth it. And I'm due a bit of good luck, surely.'

Ben nodded and wrapped his arms around her again.

'Absolutely.'

'I really think I'm falling in love with you,' Anna blurted, now that her face was squashed into him and she couldn't see his expression.

He let her go and looked into her eyes, searching. She remained steadfast, biting her lower lip, hoping against hope.

'Good,' he said gently. 'Because I'm falling in love with you.'

Anna laughed and threw herself at him, wrapping her arms around his neck.

'I think we should go on a date,' he told her.

Anna shook her head.

'I hate dating. It's awkward and tense and scary.' She smiled up at his eyes, taking his hands. 'But I would like to go on a date with you.'

'See where it takes us,' Ben added.

'Just to see what happens,' Anna agreed.

Grinning, Ben leaned down and their lips met. Anna thought it would be a quick kiss, given the onlookers and the cold, but Ben sank into it and wrapped himself about her. She did the same, pulling him closer.

The kiss was eventually broken by the sound of applause and Mr Cuthbert calling out, 'All right! Plenty of the time for that later. Some of us are cold.'

Laughing, Anna rushed back to Mr Cuthbert's car and pulled out her bag. She hugged him and then gave Maureen a hug when the woman threw up her arms at Anna.

'Thank you so much. For everything,' she told them.

'Go on.' Mr Cuthbert shooed her away, a silly grin on his face. 'Right, Maureen, let's get you home.'

Anna rushed back to Ben and threw her bag into the back of his car. He waved at Mr Cuthbert and Maureen as they got inside Mr Cuthbert's car and pulled away. Once Anna was safely in, Ben started the ignition and got the car moving again.

'Do you want to come back to mine?' he asked. 'Or should I take you back to the cottage?'

'Definitely yours,' said Anna. 'I can't stop smiling.' She laughed, her cold fingers massaging her cheeks.

Ben reached out and took her hand, giving it a squeeze. Silently, he lifted it to his lips, before dropping it so he could change gear.

Anna watched him, her heart still pounding, her mouth dry.

'Oh, before I forget,' said Ben.

'Hmm?'

'Call your mum. Her and your stepfather scare me,' said Ben, keeping his eyes on the road.

Scoffing, Anna pulled out her phone.

'Enough to scare you away?' she checked as she found her mother's number.

'Nothing in this world could do that,' said Ben, smiling as Anna put her phone to her ear and prepared herself for getting shouted at.

30

A Year Later

'Mmm, something smells good.' Ben walked into the kitchen of the Old Vicarage and kissed Anna's cheek.

'Turkey's coming on nicely,' she told him.

'I meant you,' he whispered in her ear, kissing her hair.

'No. Nope.' She held up a finger to stop him. 'I have just gotten dressed.'

'But it's tradition,' Ben pointed out, running his hands down her waist to her hips. She smacked him away playfully before turning around and wrapping her arms around him.

'We've got the rest of Christmas Day to do that,' she murmured. 'Food first, then presents while we sit on the sofa stuffed, then bed. Or the sofa. Are you going to light a fire? If we light a fire, we should stay on the sofa.'

'Oh, I'm lighting a fire. As soon as we've eaten,' said Ben, moving away and smiling at the candles Anna had prepared on the kitchen table. 'We're spending the rest of the day in the living room, wearing not a lot.' He winked at her. 'What can I do? How can I help?'

'You can't. Everything's done. Just need to wait for it to cook and stuff.'

'I think that's what the famous chefs say,' said Ben, sitting at the table. 'Wait for it to cook and stuff.'

There was a joyful pause as Anna tidied up a little and Ben watched her. The year had flown by and despite calls from parents and friends to spend their second Christmas together with others, Anna and Ben had both quickly agreed that they would spend their anniversary alone. That it was their tradition, no matter how new.

They'd had a small, heated discussion about their anniversary date. Ben had assumed it would be Boxing Day, considering everything. Anna insisted it should be the date she'd broken down outside his house and knocked on his door.

'I knew the moment I saw you,' she'd told him.

He'd scoffed.

'Then why did you go on about me being a murderer?'

'Because... Sometimes you can be wrong about whether someone is the one or not.'

In the end, they'd compromised and made their anniversary date Christmas Day. After all, that had been the best day.

'I've been thinking about this kitchen, as I've been in here so much today,' said Anna, passing Ben a glass of wine.

'I think you've spent more time in bed.'

Anna gave him a look and sat opposite him at the table.

'What would you say to a modern country style kitchen? Dark blue doors and cabinets, a wooden worktop, maybe an old vintage dresser over there and I could paint up this table, make it look different and new.'

Ben waited until Anna met his gaze.

'We agreed no work talk,' he told her.

'This isn't work talk. It's kitchen renovation talk. Our kitchen,' she hurriedly added. 'Not a client's.'

'You'd be your own client.'

'That's not how it works,' said Anna.

'That's not what you said when you redid the bathroom,' Ben reminded her. 'You said you were treating yourself as a client.'

Anna puffed out her cheeks.

'Fine. No work talk. I'll ask you again tomorrow.'

'Hmm. No,' said Ben, swallowing a mouthful of wine. 'We're visiting your mum and stepdad tomorrow.'

Anna groaned.

'Do you think it's weird they wanted to start that

tradition?'

'Not really,' said Ben, smiling. 'I think it's quite sweet. They just want to spend Christmas with you, and we said no to spending today with them. You didn't tell them why, did you?'

'No, no. Only that we wanted to make it our tradition to spend Christmas Day just the two of us. Which seems fair. Both Mum and Dad have their kids. It makes sense that we spend Christmas Eve with Dad, Boxing Day with Mum and the New Year with your family.'

'The joy of an airport at the end of December.' Ben scowled.

'It'll be fun! I love being around your family, and visiting your mum, and not just because of the sunshine and swimming pool.'

Ben laughed.

'It's nice to have a Christmas when I can show off,' Anna added quietly, sipping her wine. 'Gorgeous man who I'm now living with, flourishing business. I don't want to say it too loud, but life is good, you know?'

'We won't mention the tin of paint you upended.'

'No one ever has to know about that,' Anna told him, pointing an accusing finger. 'Leave that for the next owners to discover when they take up the carpet. And at least it was here and not at a client's house.' She downed the rest of her wine at the thought.

Ben was laughing and failing at hiding it, his

shoulders shaking as he held his glass to his lips, unable to trust filling his mouth with wine until he was sure he wouldn't choke on it.

'Next owners, huh? You're not planning on selling this place?'

Anna's eyes widened in horror.

'Oh, no. I didn't mean that. You won't sell this place ever, will you?'

Ben shook his head, standing to refill their glasses. They were going to have to slow down if they were going to enjoy their dinner.

'I was more hoping to hand it down to someone, the way my uncle passed it on to me.'

He sat and waited for Anna to meet his eyes. She smiled sweetly.

'And when would you like to make this person, or people, who will inherit?'

A pleasurable shiver ran through Ben.

'Soon,' he said. 'A year or so, maybe? I don't know.'

'A year or so sounds good,' Anna agreed.

'You're not the only one who can show off this year,' said Ben after another delightful pause, watching each other, smiles twitching at their lips. 'I get to show you off, of course, I always do. '

'Your live-in lover!'

Ben pulled a face.

'I prefer wife-to-be, but sure. And all the work you've done to the place.'

'Imagine doing interior design in Cyprus. Do you

think your mum knows people who'd like an interior designer?' asked Anna, leaning forward on the table.

'Probably. She did mention someone last time I spoke to her.'

'Really?'

'And,' said Ben, getting the conversation back on topic, 'my new job.' He sipped his wine.

Anna grinned.

'I love how proud you are,' she told him.

'Look, I know it's a step back money-wise, going freelance. But give me a couple of years and I'll have built an agency. You watch me.'

'I have no doubts,' Anna told him. 'And I love watching you.'

She stood to check on the food and Ben pulled her back until she sat on his lap.

'You're the best thing that's happened to me,' he murmured, kissing her hair, his arms around her waist. 'The best thing that ever knocked on my door.'

Anna leaned her head back on his shoulder and kissed his cheek and then the corner of his mouth.

'You're the very best thing that's ever happened to me,' she told him. She kissed his lips as he turned to her. 'You've made me so incredibly happy.'

'Good,' Ben murmured. 'Because you make me happier than I've ever been as an adult.'

Anna leaned away.

'Not as a kid?'

'Are you a Transformer? No.'

'I can make a Transformer noise,' Anna declared.

Ben leaned back and waited, unable to stop the grin on his face.

'Go on then,' he said when she didn't do anything.

Taking a deep breath, Anna made a series of clicking and whirring noises until Ben cracked up laughing.

'The happiest I've ever been as an adult,' he confirmed.

Anna laughed and kissed his lips. He held her there, until she lifted his hands from her waist and up to her breasts. He squeezed them through her thick jumper. Moaning into her lips, Ben thought through their options.

'Shall I go light the fire? So we can go in there now while we wait for everything to cook and stuff? We can eat in the living room. Move the table so we can keep an eye on it.'

'That was always an option? Why aren't we doing that?' Anna cried. 'Let's do that now.'

'Oh, but...' Ben inwardly cursed himself.

Anna didn't move. She stayed sitting on his lap, laughing at his expression.

'You know what we haven't done in a while?' she asked, standing and slowly pulling her jumper over her head. She gave a shiver. 'Brr! It's cold. You know what we haven't done?'

With a silly grin on his face, Ben asked, 'What?'

'Kitchen sex,' Anna declared, reaching around to unzip the back of her dress. 'Kitchen sex,' she announced again as she fumbled with the zip.

Ben watched her, his eyes soft, aware that he should help but too busy enjoying the show.

'Hang on,' he told her, standing and kissing her cheek. 'Sit down, don't move.'

Her brow creased, Anna did as she was told, gripping her jumper to her for warmth. Ben rushed into the living room and to the real Christmas tree in the corner, festooned with fairy lights that Anna had arranged and styled. He picked up the small box decorated in reindeer paper and rushed back to the kitchen.

'It's warmer in here than it is out there,' he murmured as the heat from the oven smacked him in the face.

'At least it's not snowing,' said Anna, smiling up at him. She'd pulled the jumper back on but held the hem, ready to remove it as soon as Ben gave her the cue. He hid the small, wrapped box behind his back.

'I know this is a cliché, but given our history, it felt right,' he started.

Anna's brow creased further and she cocked her head to the side, waiting for more.

'You make me happier than I've even been, Anna—'

'—Except for Transformers—'

'—Except for when I was a kid obsessed with

Transformers. But that kid didn't know what I know.'

Anna grinned.

'You make me so happy,' Ben reiterated. 'And I can't put into words how much I love you. How I've been in love with you since we were snowed in last Christmas. How I fell in love with you as you filled this house with your joy. How you made me and my life whole.'

Anna stared up at him, not moving, her eyes widening a little. She gasped as Ben slowly crouched down to one knee, which was exactly the reaction he'd been hoping for. He pulled out the small, wrapped box and offered it to her.

'I know we're doing presents later, but this one isn't really a present. It's a proposal.'

Anna's eyes lifted from the box to Ben.

'Will you marry me, Anna?'

Tears brimming in her eyes, Anna nodded. She gently took the box from Ben.

'Open it,' he encouraged when she seemed unsure of what to do.

'Of course I'll marry you,' she said, a quiver in her voice as she carefully unwrapped the box. The paper opened to reveal a black ring box, inside of which was a beautiful, simple diamond ring.

There was a moment of silence as Ben held his breath and then Anna squealed. Jumping up, she threw her arms around him, still down on one knee, and hugged his head to her stomach tightly. When she released him, he stood shakily and wrapped his arms around her waist, lifting her up as she kissed his face, eventually landing on his lips.

They kissed hard for a moment and then Anna pulled away to slide the ring onto her finger.

'We're engaged,' she murmured.

'We're engaged,' Ben confirmed, watching the diamond sparkle under the kitchen lights. 'See? You're my wife-to-be. We should celebrate. I bought a bottle of champagne. It's in the fridge.'

'I thought that was for our anniversary.' Anna beamed, and then she studied him. 'Go light the fire,' she told him, stepping away and removing her jumper. 'We're going to celebrate this properly.'

Ben laughed.

'Don't have to tell me twice.'

'Good. I just need to put the potatoes on,' said Anna, moving back to the oven, a new skip in her step. As Ben moved into the living room, he heard Anna calling back to him, 'Then we'll have ten minutes!'

Thank you for reading Let's Skip This Christmas. I hope you enjoyed Anna and Ben's story.
If you did, please consider leaving a rating or review wherever you get your books to help other readers find Anna and Ben.

Looking For Your Next Romance?

Try the **Christmas At The Manor** trilogy of three novellas,

Digging The Director,

Yellow Petals At Christmas

and

A Scottish Christmas Dream

by Jennifer Nice.

Find your next read at
www.writeintothewoods.com/romance